MotoRaid

Keith Thye

Elfin Cove Press
Seattle, Washington

ELFIN COVE PRESS
914 Virginia St.
Seattle, WA 98101

Project manager: Bernie Kuntz
Cover design: Dave Marty
Text design: Laurel Strand

Library of Congress 99-072751

ISBN 0-944958-48-6

Printed in the United States of America
1   3   5   7   9   10   8   6   4   2

prologue

The cell was dank, dark, and very cold. A light bulb dangling from the ceiling illuminated my surroundings — a single cot stretched against one wall and a broken toilet.

Hunched on the dirt floor, separated from Dave by the thick walls, I reflected on our plight and felt only desperation. Though I was confident that officials from the U.S. Embassy in Lima would get us released, we first had to persuade the Peruvian guards to allow us a phone call. A full day had passed, and still they ignored us. We had heard that the Peruvians treated suspected drug smugglers with complete disdain. We were finding out just how true that was.

chapter one

U.S.A.

The weather was cold that first day on our road to adventure. At least it wasn't wet, as Oregon usually is in late January.

The motorcycles had been packed for days and stood waiting for us. At 6 a.m. on January 26, 1963, we mounted the bikes and pulled out of Lake Oswego with a destination in southern Chile. The temperature hovered at twenty-five degrees and did not seem to improve as the day progressed. The first spurt of sixty miles proved to us that we were not accustomed to riding in subfreezing temperatures. But we soon learned to travel in thirty-mile runs so that we would not get too cold. We arrived in Eugene, Oregon, by 9 a.m. and spent several hours warming up at the Sigma Phi Epsilon fraternity house. As much as anything, we received moral support, for here was where this trip really began.

My father had immigrated to the United States from Denmark when he was twenty-one, and I enjoyed listening to his stories of the trials and tribulations of adapting to a new land and people.

He couldn't speak a word of English when he arrived in America, and the first few years were difficult as he adjusted to his new life. When he spoke of these times, however, his eyes would light up with an excitement that had long since passed from his everyday life. His stories were intertwined with comments of the intrigue and adventure he had experienced. As he would unravel his stories to me and my older brother Gary, I would dream of someday having my own adventure.

I was a senior in high school when Gary and two friends left for a long summer vacation of touring Europe on motor scooters. When he returned to continue his university studies, we would get together and he would tempt my wanderlust by reliving some of his European experiences. Gary and I were always very close, and he knew that he was kindling my passion for adventure.

As a freshman at the University of Oregon, I began thinking about a trip that would be a little different from the European journey that my brother had experienced. I was looking for an exploit that few people had attempted — an adventure with an element of the unusual. I don't know when I first thought about a motorcycle trip through Central and South America, but I do know that the more I thought about the idea, the better I liked it.

As the idea developed in my mind, I began talking to friends in an effort to recruit companions. Most of the fellows in the fraternity house at one time or another were planning or at least seriously thinking about joining me on the journey. But all eventually changed their minds. The requirements of time and money were more than anyone was willing to commit to.

In January of 1962, one year before my planned departure, I was getting concerned. Not wanting to do this trip alone, I approached everyone who might be ready, willing, and able. Actually, everyone was ready, willing, and able but nobody would commit. Until I called Dave Yaden.

Dave was an old high school buddy of mine. We had played together in a dance band for about six years. I had not previously called Dave because he was a straight "A" student at Portland State and I really didn't think he would drop out of school for a year. I remember the Sunday night when I called: "Hi, Dave. It's Keith."

"Hey man, what's happening?"

"Listen, I'm going to South America on a motorcycle next year and I need a traveling companion."

"I'm on."

"No, listen, I'm serious. This thing is going to take about a year. You'll have to drop out of school, work, earn money. Seriously."

"I'm telling you, I'm on."

And with that it started. We began saving the money from our gigs. When our sophomore year was over, we both acquired well-paying jobs in the local sawmills and concentrated on planning and saving for the ensuing year. And we needed a full year to plan this adventure. Money was only part of it. We each had exactly $1,200 that cold day in January when we headed out. We thought it would be enough.

The year of planning was consumed by writing to every agency we could think of and gathering information on climate, culture, maps, fuel availability, food, languages, and dialects. We tried to think of everything. We needed passports, visas for each country of visitation, and most difficult of all, a customs carnet.

We discovered, well into the planning stage, that the customs carnet was required before the countries of South America would allow us to bring in a vehicle. This document was not necessary for travel through the countries of Central America.

The economies of the nations of South America were in a delicate balance, teetering on the brink of complete ruination. They were attempting to control inflation and the monetary system through a set of price controls. The black market was doing "land office" business, seriously affecting the various governments' attempts to stabilize the legitimate market. The governments, therefore, had to control the goods and services entering the economies.

The customs carnet was a cash bond that had to be advanced prior to taking a vehicle into South America. The governments were concerned that individuals would purchase vehicles elsewhere and dump them in South American countries at greatly inflated prices. Upon returning the vehicle to the country of origin, the customs carnet was supposed to be refunded. We were skeptical about ever getting our money back, but we did eventually recover the bond. And it was sizable — $1,000 for a used vehicle of about half that value.

The other portion of the planning revolved around what to take with us. There is not room on a motorcycle for much more than the essentials for living and maintaining the bikes, so the question of what to take and what to leave was ever-present. Clothing had to include adequate protection for both hot and cold climates, rain and sun. We would be cooking our own meals and therefore needed all the utensils, as well as water purification systems. Sleeping bags and a good, lightweight tent for sleeping were essential. Spare parts were necessary, for we knew repair shops would be few and far between.

The other problem was how to carry and secure our gear. We would often be leaving the bikes parked while wandering about, and we did not want our belongings to disappear.

We eventually designed and had constructed steel boxes with hinged lids, which we bolted to the frame at the rear of each bike, on either side of the wheel, like saddlebags. Although awkward looking and terribly weighty, with heavy-duty shocks the arrangement seemed to work.

We bought the bikes one year in advance. Deciding the make of motorcycles was really no contest. Our hearts were set on BMW R-50 machines because of their ruggedness and reliability. Also, repair shops were located in the major cities of Central and South America and we knew that there would be occasional problems. Japanese bikes were just beginning to infiltrate the U.S. marketplace. Most bikes of the time were Harley-Davidsons or various English and Italian makes, but none of these manufacturers had well-established international service networks.

Having made this decision, we searched for, and found, two used motorcycles that fit our requirements. We paid $800 each for them. Although both were a couple of years old with about 30,000 miles, we had no doubt that these machines would suit us well. Whenever we got a few days off from working, we set off on short "training-run" excursions.

One trip to British Columbia was particularly memorable. As we approached Everett, Washington, about eighty miles south of the Canadian border, a ferocious wind kicked up and was coming at us from "eleven o'clock." Dave was leading the way and leaning hard to the left into the wind, and I was doing the same several hundred yards behind.

All of a sudden, he bolted across the center line into the on-coming lane of traffic. Fortunately, there was a space several car lengths long. He shot clear through that and ended up on the southbound lanes' shoulder. Naturally, I backed way off. When I arrived at the spot where Dave had lost control, my bike shot forward. Apparently, the storm had created a vacuum-like air pocket.

From Vancouver, we headed east on Highway 3 through Hope and Princeton, British Columbia. Just short of Osoyoos, where we intended crossing back into the United States, we had a major problem. Again, Dave was running ahead of me, about fifty yards this time. We were clipping along at sixty-five miles per hour. There was no shoulder on our side of the road. Instead, a fruit orchard came nearly to the edge of the pavement.

It happened fast, so fast I don't remember the details. I do recall staring straight into the eyes of a German Shepherd that must have weighed 150 pounds. Apparently, he was in the orchard and had seen or heard the first bike go by. He charged out onto the pavement to make pursuit without knowing I was coming. I drilled him right in the ribs.

I remember the awful sensation of flying over the handlebars and throwing out my hands to cushion the blow when my body hit the pavement. The three of us (the dog, the bike, and myself) slid, spiraling down the pavement for about sixty or seventy yards. The dog suffered the worst. He managed to get up and limp, howling all the way, back into the orchard. We caught up with his owner later and learned that, although the dog was suffering from several broken bones, he was expected to recover.

Fortunately, although the temperature rose to ninety degrees that day, I was protectively dressed: Navy pea jacket, gloves, heavy jeans, and a helmet. The helmet took most of the impact. All that held it together was the webbing on the inside. I got beat up a fair amount myself — scraped my hands and face, but no broken bones.

The bike was a little worse for wear. A steel rod surrounds the most vulnerable parts of the engine in case of a crash; hence the term "crash bar." The crash bar was destroyed and the headlight was in about three pieces, all dangling by wires from its mount on the handlebars. The BMW had horizontal cylinders that stuck out from the side of the bike. As the bike slid down the pavement on its side, it wore a silver-dollar-sized hole in the valve cover on the end of the cylinder head.

Dave didn't see the accident, but once he realized I was no longer following him, he returned to find out what had happened to me. I was sitting up against one of the fruit trees, nursing my wounds. The dog was long gone by this time. After determining that I was all right to ride, we kicked the front wheel into alignment and headed into Osoyoos. Although it was a Sunday, we found a gas station with a mechanic doing some work on his own car. He sheared off part of the side of a coffee can, secured it over the valve cover hole with some gasket sealant and six screws, and sent us on our way. The bike was incapable of high speeds because of the alignment; quite frankly, I didn't feel like speed myself. So we limped along. As darkness fell, I had to ride very close behind Dave, because my headlight was shining straight down onto my front axle. We eventually made it home late that night and immediately began to plan our next excursion. I have to admit, though, that about two weeks passed before my body had recuperated to the point where I felt like climbing onto the saddle again.

And so it went. We made these frequent two- and three-day outings in order to get fully acquainted with the machines and our equipment.

That January day on which we embarked was too cold for any comfort on a motorcycle. As we approached San Francisco two days later, it started getting wet as well. We were about thirty miles from the city, and darkness had long since fallen. Traffic was heavy and fast and suddenly we were at the toll booth of the Benicia Bridge. Decked out in our rubber rainsuits, we had to half undress to get at some money. All the while, cars were piling up behind us, honking their horns.

My brother Gary was living in the area and was gracious enough to put us up for several days. We needed some time to acquire visas from all the Latin Republic Consulates. Most of them are located in fairly close proximity on Market Street in downtown San Francisco. That was a help because they all have different hours, and we would have to make several stops to secure the necessary documents. These consulates held irregular schedules that often did not match the posted hours. After two frustrating days, we finally managed to secure all the proper documents except for our customs carnets, which we did not expect for several days.

With sixteen visas in hand, we left for Los Angeles, our next major destination. We had hoped to make the four hundred miles in one day, but we left San Francisco in a downpour with heavy winds. Though warned of extensive flooding, we were anxious to get moving. The torrent continued, intensifying as we pushed south. In Salinas, which received five inches of rain that day, the streets were flooded so badly that we drove down the sidewalks to get through town.

Back on the highway, we hit one low spot that sent water cascading over the handlebars. It was a miserable day, and we managed only half the distance we had hoped for. Furthermore, we had to spend the night in a motel, an expense we had not included in our budget.

The next day continued wet. The heavy rains we had experienced the previous day, however, subsided. Our drive to Los Angeles was slow because of the wet conditions, but the highway flooding had disappeared.

A friend of ours from high school lived in La Habra and offered us space in his apartment for several days while we waited for our remaining documents and took sightseeing junkets all around Los Angeles.

The situation at the apartment was a bit strained. Our friend Steve roomed with two brothers. Bob was the self-proclaimed "greatest surfer in the world," while Jake was quite proud of claiming title to the fastest set of wheels in La Habra. Their egos made a tight situation out of the crowded two-bedroom apartment.

But matters got worse. Julie, Jinnie, and Barbara lived across the court. Julie was a nice-looking, pleasant girl. Jinnie was barely attractive and skinny as a beanpole. She tried very hard to please everyone by being motherly. Barbara was robust and extremely disagreeable. It didn't take long to figure out that there was some sort of round robin going on. Dave and I had laid out our sleeping bags on the living room floor, but we weren't getting much sleep. These girls kept coming and going all night, sometimes tripping over us trying to get from room to room. Just observing their activity for four days was enough to tire me out.

About six in the morning one day, Dave was standing in the middle of the front room stark naked, bending over to put on his shorts. Barbara came bolting out of Bob's room and, startled upon seeing Dave standing there, tripped and fell directly into him. As a spectator to this event, I am not sure which I enjoyed more — watching Dave trying to get out from under her or watching Barbara trying to stay on top of him.

This awkward event started an unusual day. We were stopped three times by cops. The first was merely curious about the huge metal boxes we had bolted to the bikes. The second one nailed us for speeding but, because we were from out of state, did not ticket us. And the third one kicked us out of someone's swimming pool. I later found out our hosts did not really know the homeowners.

Sitting around for several days waiting for mail to arrive can be frustrating. Finally, we began calling daily to find out where our customs carnets were. On Saturday, we learned they were at the post office, which was closed, of course. No matter. We went down and banged on the door until someone answered. With packet in hand, we went immediately to the apartment to start packing. We were ready to begin our adventure.

• • •

No rain had fallen in Los Angeles for 312 days. When Dave and I decided to leave town, however, the drought ended with a vengeance. We didn't care, for we were on our way to Mexico. But we did not get there that night. Among other problems, I broke my primer needle, which controls the flow of fuel to the carburetor, and fixed it with a paper clip found alongside the road.

We spent the night about three miles from the border, curled up in our sleeping bags in our tent with a hard rain falling all night long. The rain wasn't what kept us awake, though. We had pitched down in a farmer's field by the side of an irrigation ditch next to a power pole. We hadn't noticed at the time, but the pole emitted a low, ghostly growl that rose and fell in pitch and loudness. Spooky!

That night, I thought what a great mental pacifier a tent can be. A thin sheeting of canvas between oneself and the darkness outside, a candle to read by, and a sleeping bag to keep warm. Although far from secure, it gives a tremendous feeling of safety.

chapter two

Mexico

Entering Mexico was not a problem. The border officials asked only to see our tourist visas.

The contrast of crossing the border struck us immediately. Mexicali, on the Mexican side of the border, sharply contrasted to Los Angeles and the desert towns through which we had just traveled. It was a filthy conglomeration of stucco shacks with most of the windows boarded up with plywood and cardboard. Weeds grew between the cracks in the structures, giving a deserted feeling to the town. Though depressing at first, we soon grew accustomed to it.

We rode about two hundred miles into Mexico, making frequent stops at the small, weather-beaten towns along the way. There wasn't much to do or anything we needed to accomplish in these towns, but we wanted to get a feel for the people and practice our Spanish a bit. Dave was fluent in the language, having studied it in school. I took a crash course before leaving on the trip and understood it fairly well, but was not much good at speaking it.

We considered this to be the true first day of our adventure. Although we had traveled nearly 3,000 miles so far (with all of our running around in the cities), we did not consider the trip officially started until we were on foreign soil. From this point forth, we had no timetable. We expected to reach Chile sometime in June, but had left the date open.

Our hometown of Lake Oswego, Oregon, had developed a sister-city relationship with Pucón, Chile, a few years earlier. This cultural exchange program had received a fair amount of coverage in the local papers. Pucón is approximately the same number of degrees south of the equator as Lake Oswego is north, so comparisons between the climates of the two cities were emphasized. These articles sparked our interest and helped set South America — Chile, in particular — as our destination.

A few people had exchanged visits between the two cities, but no one had attempted the journey by land. We did not know what to anticipate along the way and therefore had no idea of how long the journey would take. What's more, we really didn't care. Our only limitation was the amount of money we had. We expected to return in time for fall term in late September, but even this was subject to change.

The first night in Mexico, we pulled off the highway and ventured about half a mile into the desert before making camp. We had heard that some bad hombres lived in the desert mountains. The last thing we wanted to be was conspicuous. So we pulled well off the road about an hour before sunset and set up camp, making sure our cooking fire was extinguished before total darkness fell.

Our accommodations frequently consisted of our mountain tent and two sleeping bags. We usually pulled well off the road and into the countryside to establish camp.

There wasn't much to our camp. We had a lightweight mountain tent that was pretty snug for the two of us. Our two sleeping bags just barely fit inside. The tent was easy to assemble, with a rugged, rubberized canvas floor and two poles for support. The front pole was constructed of three one-foot pieces, each piece fitting snugly into the next for solid support. The foot of the tent was supported by a single one-foot-long pole. The tent was ideal because it was small, lightweight, and rolled into a tight cylinder.

We usually parked the bikes on either side of the tent so that we would hear any activity near them. Occasionally, when we would park for the night somewhere we did not feel comfortable, we tied one end of a thin nylon rope to the wheels and secured the other end to the tent pole. Anyone trying to take the bikes would certainly attract our attention.

Awakening our first morning in Mexico was exhilarating, for no reason other than that we were where we wanted to be. We traveled a few short miles down the road and were stopped by a customs inspector. As luck would have it, we had not collected the proper permits for the cycles at the border and had to back-track about forty miles to Sonoyta to resolve the matter. We thought getting into Mexico had been too easy, and our intuition had been confirmed.

The Mexican road was a pleasure, paved all the way and in fairly good shape. High rates of speed in the open desert were common, and traffic was nearly nonexistent.

Our biggest problem was avoiding stray cows that would wander onto the roadway. Through the desert, the road was straight and a bit like a roller coaster. The arroyos were not worth building bridges over, so the road would dip abruptly into these dry creek beds. Cows often looked there for moisture or vegetation. If they happened to be standing in the road, it could be nerve-wracking. We would come flying off the lip of the dip, often becoming slightly airborne. If a cow had ever been directly in the way, I probably would not be writing this. No hits, but some near misses.

We had been in Mexico for three days and had spent a total of $5.70 apiece. Gasoline cost about thirty cents per gallon. We bought our food along the way in small markets or at roadside stands and prepared it over an open fire. With a tight budget, our needs were simple.

We headed south to Hermosillo and then on through Guaymas and Ciudad Obregón. Moving toward the interior and out of the

Our side trips to remote villages often took us away from established roads. Many of these settlements could be reached only by footpaths.

desert, things seemed to get better in every respect. The environment became greener, and therefore, more people were to be found. They appeared more gregarious and prosperous, exuding a pleasantness we had not previously encountered. The weather improved as well, and brilliant cloudless skies became the norm.

We stopped at a little cafe in the central park of Mazatlán and ordered some tacos. Since we were back in civilization, we decided to act civilized. The tacos were served with plastic forks so naturally, being civilized, I picked up a fork and began to attack my taco. When I pressed on it, the fork snapped in half and the prong end flipped over onto the next table, surprising my neighboring diner. I became embarrassed as everyone in the packed place began staring and laughing. We brought the house down, however, when Dave picked up his plastic fork and tried to begin eating his taco. His fork snapped with such force that half of it flew clear across the cafe. From that point forth, we ate with our hands.

The fork episode was an omen of sorts. We both were up most of the night with the dry heaves.

The next morning, as we were climbing the bank out of our creek bed, I tipped over my cycle. No damage to speak of, but I had to repack everything. Then we started down the highway.

There is an old adage that you can always tell a motorcycle rider by the bugs in his teeth. Sometimes, it's quite true. Just a few kilometers down the road, we passed through a swarm of bees. One managed to get inside Dave's shirt. By the time he got the bike stopped and his shirt off, he looked like he had measles on his back.

We crossed the Tropic of Cancer (which marks the northern boundary of the tropics) in the afternoon and headed into the interior of Mexico. The weather turned hot. We attempted to ride in shirtsleeves, but protecting ourselves from the sun became a constant battle. We used a heavy lotion on our arms, torsos, and faces and white lotion on sensitive areas, such as our noses.

With the beards we had begun to grow, we looked a little ridiculous. My beard was red and fairly full. Dave's, however, was a sight to see, growing as it did in random splotches. For some reason, he let these sections continue to grow. Several months later, he somewhat resembled one of those Chinese men who deliberately cultivate strategically located strands of long hair. Dave's problem was that his beard grew in haphazard clumps. Quite a sight!

We got a slow start leaving Mazatlán, yet we hoped to reach

Guadalajara that evening. But we fouled up, or more appropri-
ately, we had been fouled up all along and just had not realized it.
We got to talking to some Mexican acquaintances and discovered
that we had crossed into a different time zone at Mexicali and
should have set our watches forward one hour. Furthermore, we
would cross into another time zone and lose one more hour before
arriving at Guadalajara. We gunned it and arrived in Guadalajara
late that evening. We got our first motel room, and therefore our
first shower, since Los Angeles. But the twenty pesos ($1.60) apiece
for the room gave us guilty consciences regarding our budget.

From Guadalajara to Mexico City is well over four hundred
miles, and we wanted to make that distance the next day. We
pushed hard all day long. About one hundred miles from Mexico
City, we climbed into the mountains. We had been using regular
gas, and when the bikes got above 6,000 feet, they began to run
rough. We had to stop several times to adjust our carburetors.

The mountains were beautiful, but tough — steep inclines and
one hundred miles of horseshoe curves, one right after another.
Being pressed for time, we were barreling into these turns. I was
going first and came flying into a sharp right-hand curve. I didn't
see the oil slick before I hit it — just caught the edge and began to
fishtail wildly. Dave saw me sliding all over and had just enough
time to swear before he plowed straight into the slick. He set his
bike down hard on the right side and slid across the road into the
ditch on the far side. In the meantime, I was careening down the
road doing my best to keep my bike upright. I ended up on the
gravel shoulder, but fortunately did not tip over.

Dave was pretty well banged up. His right hand and shoulder

were scraped, but we managed to patch him up. The bike had some scratches, but the crash bar protecting the engine had done its job. We limped into Mexico City that night and looked up a friend who was expecting us.

A couple of days in Mexico City gave us a chance to do some sightseeing and, more importantly, to get the bikes fixed. We found the local BMW dealer and left Dave's bike first. It took two days to fix his and one to tune mine. In the meantime, we rode double on the available unit.

Mexico City is a beautiful city with many squares and statues, but as a planned urban development, it has a problem. Most of the main streets run at diagonals to one another and meet at the statues, creating traffic circles with numerous spokes. Traffic is disorganized, and drivers are unpredictable. There are no lane lines on the streets, and vehicles continually cut in and out, often changing four or five lanes without looking. Add pedestrians stepping into the street at any point, and the scene is set for some tense driving situations. But we were not the only two-wheelers. Motor scooters were everywhere, although larger motorcycles were rare.

Back on the road, we found ourselves in the desert again, except this time at an elevation of 8,000 feet. The bikes were running well at this altitude now, and we were making good time. What slowed us down was some sort of rash I developed which left hundreds of large bumps all over my body. They did not itch, but occasionally one would break and bleed. I intended to find a doctor, but by the time we reached Oaxaca the condition had disappeared.

The country turned beautiful. High alpine forests covered the slopes, and the road snaked through groves of majestic pine trees. The paved road rose to 10,000 feet and then dropped back down to more moderate elevations. As the day progressed, the altitude continued to drop. In the course of one day, we experienced transitions from arid to semiarid to high forests to semitropical.

As we passed through the countryside, we stopped to talk to people along the side of the road – farmers, road crews, students waiting for buses. This particular day, we met a group of cane cutters. The primary agricultural resource in the area was sugar cane, and the men would set off early in the morning with their machetes. Seeing them walking down the road with two-foot-long knives and axes led one to wonder if stopping and talking was a wise thing to do. We found that the farther south we went in Mexico, the meaner they looked and yet the friendlier they became. We did not have a chance to become friends with any individuals, but we certainly learned to like the people of the area as a group.

We had been on the road for just one month when "Black Sunday" arrived. We arose from our crude campsite and got back on the road by midmorning. Clouds lingered for awhile, and then the weather became clear and hot near Tuxtla Gutiérrez. We entered the mountains again and seemed to climb forever. The pass peaked at 10,500 feet, and then we began the descent. Many of the inhabitants here were true mountain Indians, looking almost Chinese and speaking their own dialects. Being Sunday, they were all dressed in their most colorful clothes.

About four o'clock that afternoon, we arrived in Comitán. I knew I had a problem with my clutch for it was making a weird snapping sound and was becoming hard to shift. I hoped to reach Guatemala City, however, where repairs could be made. We stopped for a bite to eat and met two Danish fellows who were trying to get to Guatemala City in a beat-up Volkswagen bus. We learned later that the VW gave up on them in Guatemala City and they returned to Mexico City by bus.

About three miles out of Tuxtla Chico, my bike broke down. We assumed it was the clutch. At any rate, the bike was not drivable, at least not under its own power.

Since it was getting late, we decided to camp where the breakdown occurred. By the time we got around to pitching the tent, darkness had fallen. Consequently, we did not do a thorough job of setting the tent.

That was a mistake. The rain began, turning into a downpour around midnight. Since the tent was not tight, water collected in puddles on the canvas and started to leak through. It started slowly, and soon — with the deluge outside — we felt like we were lying in a shower. Then the wind kicked up and grabbed hold of the wet canvas, yanking the tent from its moorings. Had we not been inside the tent, it surely would have blown away. All we could do was continue to lie within the collapsed tent as the rain and wind beat on us all night long. We finally managed to fall asleep, soaked and uncomfortable. When we awoke, the sky was clear.

We had discussed our plight throughout the evening and decided that having the bike hauled back to Mexico City would be a mistake. The road was long, and besides, we would have to backtrack. We were headed to Guatemala City, and since it was closer than Mexico City we decided to have the bikes transported there.

The next morning, Dave returned to Comitán to arrange for a truck while I stayed at the camp with my motorcycle. Three hours passed before he returned with the transporter, which was fine because I needed that long to clean up the mess left over from the storm.

Getting my bike on the truck was tough because there were only three of us to push the vehicle up a very steep board inclining from the ground onto the truck.

We climbed into the truck's cab and headed for the Guatemala border, about fifty miles away. When we got to the border, the driver stopped the truck, got out, went around to the back of the truck, and beckoned for us to join him.

We asked, "What are you doing?"

He replied, "I go no further. Help me get the bike down."

We said, "Wait a minute. You told us you would take us to Guatemala City. You know that we have a machine here that is not operable."

He said, "I told you I would take you to Guatemala, not Guatemala City. I can't cross into the country because I have no official document. As a matter of fact, there is no interstate trucking here."

Fortunately for us, we had paid him only part of the money we had negotiated.

We took the bike off the truck and then contemplated what to do. We were now fifty miles farther south from the point at which we had faced this same problem.

It was about 150 miles to Guatemala City and a repair shop, so we decided to tow my bike behind Dave's. When we made that decision, however, we had no idea what lay ahead.

chapter three

Guatemala

First, we had to officially cross the border from Mexico into Guatemala. We later figured out that, for some unknown reason, border crossings were always difficult. There would be the main customs station at the border itself and then several more checkpoints within the next few miles.

Guards at each of the checkpoints insisted on restamping and verifying all the documents from the previous checkpoint. It was not uncommon for a guard at any one of the customs stations to try to intimidate us or to solicit a bribe in order to let us continue.

This first customs station, though it was on the Pan-American Highway, was fairly desolate. Except for the truck that had brought us (now on its way back to Comitán), we saw no other vehicles. The border guard insisted that we pay approximately ten dollars apiece to continue. Of course, we refused. He kept fingering the pistol that was holstered at his side. We tried a tactic that was successful in this case and would be useful in future situations as well. We insisted on seeing his official government employee card and made a big issue of recording his customs badge number. Once a guard discovered we would report his actions to his superiors, he would allow us to pass — usually.

We had been carrying fifty feet of thin but very strong nylon rope. We tied one end to the rear of Dave's cycle and the other end to the neck of my front assembly, just below the handlebars. He was going to tow about 1,000 pounds, including the bike, the equipment, and myself, so we doubled the rope, leaving a gap of about twenty feet between us. What we did not know was that the next hundred miles was all dirt road.

We had become spoiled with the condition of the Pan-American Highway in Mexico. It was paved all the way and kept in good repair. Sections of it needed repair and road crews were working on some parts, but generally the road allowed us to sustain reasonable speed. That all changed when we crossed into Guatemala.

The 100-mile stretch on which we were about to embark was called the El Tapon landslide area. The highway was nothing more than a dirt lane carved out of the mountainside, following every bend in the river below. There were precipitous drops into the river almost the entire distance. And, of course, landslides were common. The road itself was awful. Huge chuckholes pockmarked the roadbed, making travel extremely slow, especially on two wheels. Additionally, boulders that had rolled off the mountainside lay all over the road. The highway was no wider than a one-lane road for most of the distance. We understood now why there was no international commerce.

Dave started his motorcycle, and I climbed on mine. He inched ahead slowly until the rope was taut between us. As he began to

The El Tapon landslide area through northern Guatemala was rough on us and the bikes. Dave towed my disabled motorcycle for several days. The rope can be seen stretching between the two machines.

put the power to his machine, we got an idea of just what a pull this would be. We were on a level part of the dirt road. Slowly, my bike began to follow. Dave had to keep his bike in first gear, which restricted our speed to about twenty miles per hour. But most of the time, we could not go even that fast.

I didn't know how miserable a body could feel until that day ended. The road was gruesome and required constant attention as we dodged the chuckholes and boulders. The area was very dry, and the dust that Dave kicked up hit me directly in the face. I soon realized that I needed a wet towel over my face to protect myself from the dust. But clean water, which we each carried with us in two-gallon cans, was a precious commodity, and we had no idea how many days this would take.

The towing went well as long as we were on level ground. The problem was that the road dipped up and down as it snaked along the river. The uphill portions were particularly hard on Dave's machine, straining his engine, clutch, and rear shock absorbers. The downhill stretches were even worse.

Dave tried to keep a constant speed going downhill, and I tried to do the same. But as he dodged the chuckholes and boulders, we would get a little slack in the rope between us. Then, one of two things would happen. Either we would both get jolted as the rope became taut again, or the rope would get more slack. When this happened, the slack would touch my front wheel, and in an instant the rope would wrap around the axle. The first time this happened, we were caught completely by surprise. Both bikes jerked hard as the rope stretched taut, and there was no way we could stay on. We managed to jump off just before the bikes crashed into the dirt.

After that, I tended to ride my brakes hard on the downhill stretches. Still, we occasionally would have this problem. It got to the point where I would yell, "Jump!" and we would immediately bail off and let the bikes crash.

We covered only forty miles that day and were beginning to wonder if the cycles could survive the punishment. We had not seen another vehicle all day long, or even people for that matter, and realized how desolate our position was.

We camped along the side of the road that night and had only a cup of soup for dinner. We were too exhausted to prepare anything else. Expecting to have been in Guatemala City by this time, we had not provisioned ourselves for extra days. The wind had started to blow hard in the early afternoon, and by evening it was howling so hard we had a difficult time getting the campstove lit.

Apparently, the last batch of water we got was bad, for that night I became ill. We had been using a water purification system, but had been told before we started our journey that it is still possible to get sick. On top of that, my eyes were killing me from the dust flying in my face throughout the afternoon. I spent a sleepless night.

The next morning, as we were taking down our campsite, we heard an engine. A Canadian of Swiss extraction was traveling alone in a Volkswagen, trying to get to Guatemala City. He stopped and shared some of his fruit with us. He was a nice fellow, but he certainly was upset at that moment.

He had decided to get an early start that day, arriving at the customs station at dawn. Being alone, he did not have a chance against the border guard. It sounded like the same one who had confronted us. The guard confiscated his watch and all his cash before allowing him passage. This guy was visibly shaking, he was so upset. He was even considering returning to the border with physical harm in mind, thinking he could get the upper hand with a surprise attack.

After breakfast, we said goodbye to our Canadian friend, and he left a few minutes before our own departure. As he drove off, Dave and I talked about our emotional state, and we found we both felt the same depression. Spending another day of fighting the road tied together by our tow rope was the last thing in the world we wanted to do. Furthermore, we had just seen our friend drive off in relative luxury. Nonetheless, we rigged the bikes up as we had the day before and climbed back into the saddle for another long day.

Two hours into our journey, we rounded a curve in the road and found the Canadian sitting on the rear bumper of his VW. In front of him was a recent rock slide. He said that when he got there, dust was still settling from the slide. It was about seventy-five feet from one end to the other and nearly covered the width of the road. Dave and I determined we could push our bikes along the precipice edge if we kicked a few rocks into the river below.

Venturing onto the landslide and pushing the rocks over the brink was risky, however, for the mass of dirt and rock was unstable. Cautiously, we accomplished the task. Then we needed to get the bikes across. The wheels of the bikes would be right at the edge of the road, which fell steeply about a hundred feet to the river. The problem was where to walk as we pushed the bikes across.

Our friend in the VW was out of luck. We tried to figure a way to get the car across the slide, but it simply was not possible. As he drove back toward the Mexican border, we wondered what type of confrontation he would have with the border guard.

Because of the delay in getting around the landslide, we were forced to spend a second night in the El Tapon area. By late afternoon, as we approached civilization, the road improved. We picked up some fruit and canned goods at a small village. In the last two days, we had eaten only the Canadian's fruit and a few cups of soup.

During the day, my illness had turned to dysentery. After we stopped for the night, I spent more time out of the sleeping bag than inside. I fell asleep for short periods, awaking to tremendous cramps in my stomach which curled me up into a ball.

The night progressed with frequent trips from the tent to the nearby field. There wasn't much foliage around the tent, but I didn't care, at least until morning came. Again, I was awakened by a severe cramp. When the worst had passed, I darted from the tent and squatted in the field, about ten yards from the tent. I had been doing this all night long, but now it was daylight. What I had not realized was that I had been running from the tent toward the road. Whoever would have thought that a school bus full of students would be passing by at 6 a.m.? There was no place to hide, so I just watched them from my squat as they watched me from their bus. They were pointing at me and laughing and slapping each other on the back as the bus rolled out of sight.

We cleared up our campsite, got the bikes loaded and tied together, and headed down the road toward Quetzaltenango. The road improved significantly, even turning to pavement after a short distance, which facilitated our towing. The countryside was becoming lush, with a semitropical flavor to it. I wished I could have enjoyed it, but with dysentery and the problems encountered with towing I just wanted to reach our destination and lie down. We passed through San Cristobal where we found a gas station and refueled Dave's bike, and then finished the twelve miles or so into Quetzaltenango.

I needed to rest for a day or two, and Dave was beginning to feel queasy as well. With the extensive repairs needed on our bikes, we didn't want to spend much for a room. We found one for seventy-five cents apiece per day. You get what you pay for. We had no hot water and the only bathroom was communally shared, but after my first trip to the john, I think we had it all to ourselves.

The following day my condition improved, but Dave was feeling worse. We decided, however, that we would keep on for Guatemala City. Our bikes would be in the shop for several days, giving us plenty of time to recuperate.

We found a trucking firm that would haul my motorcycle to the BMW shop in Guatemala City. The truck would not be leaving until late in the afternoon, so Dave and I rode around Quetzaltenango on his bike. It struck me that the Mexican women had been much more attractive than the Guatemalan women. The Guatemalans seemed to be featureless in comparison. They made no effort to show off their beauty; rather, they went out of their way to hide it. Both groups, however, dressed in colorful dresses. The men seemed to compare similarly between the two nations.

One thing was very obvious: in both countries, there were two distinct classes of people — those with and those without. Members of the elite class had little to do with the peasants, even going out of their way to avoid contact. We were in a position where we could enjoy both classes. We lived with the peasants but were accepted by the upper class as well. We enjoyed both.

At two o'clock that afternoon, we spotted a guy standing across the park from us who obviously was a tourist — crew cut, beret, wild Guatemalan sweater with about forty colors in it, and brand-new sandals. His name was Walt Zucker, and he was traveling through Central America by bus. We asked how he had gotten through the El Tapon landslide, and he said he had hitchhiked from the border with two Danish guys in a VW bus. Obviously, they had crossed before the landslide struck.

Walt was pleased to be able to ride with me in the truck into Guatemala City. In the meantime, Dave cycled off alone for the 130-mile ride to the city in order to set up a room for us. By the time I caught up with him, he was feeling as sick as I had several days earlier.

Our days in Guatemala City were very memorable. We left the bikes in the shop one at a time so we would have transportation. While my bike was being fixed, I rode Dave's cycle all over town. Dysentery hit him hard the first two days, and he spent most of his time in the hotel room.

We met two missionaries staying across the hall from our room, and they pointed out the sights to see, both in the city itself and in the countryside. It took five days to get both bikes fixed. In the meantime, we saw all the city's many attractions.

One problem we had was our wash. Laundromats were non-existent, and the places we stayed had no washers or dryers. When we were on the road, we would jump into the nearest stream with our clothes on and with any dirty laundry we had, then hang it to dry over shrubs or lines tied between the bikes. In the cities, we had to hand-wash as best we could, usually over a rough surface of some sort, and then hang-dry. Our clothes were showing the abuse.

These periods when we stayed in the major cities were good opportunities for us to catch up on necessary tasks. We wrote letters to people back home and stopped by the U.S. consulate or embassy to pick up mail. We looked up the consulates of the next countries to be visited in order to get our visas authorized. Also, since we were shooting lots of pictures, we took our cameras in for cleaning. We did not want dust to get into the lenses and cloud the pictures.

Eager to get back on the road, we loaded our repaired bikes with provisions and headed for the country. First we rode northwest for Lake Atitlán, about forty miles from Guatemala City.

The map showed a straight and paved road. Well, it was paved, but certainly not straight. The road wound around, up, and down some of the steepest canyon walls we had seen. We arrived at the lake at dusk. Looking down from the road, the scenery was beautiful. The moonlight shone on the water, and some fog formed on the surface.

At each end of the lake, a majestic volcano rose to heights of nearly 10,000 feet. The two volcanoes, San Pedro and Tolimán, began to collect heavy cloud formations around their peaks, which enhanced the view from our vantage point. That night, we stayed on the lakeshore, near Panajachel.

The next morning was overcast and it looked like it might rain. We rode the bikes across old dusty trails that bumped across the countryside, resembling cow paths more than roads. It was only about ten miles, however, to Chichicastenango where, being a Thursday, the fair was in full swing. The market was situated in the town square between two churches, and we arrived at the appropriate hour. What a colorful sight! The men were dressed in white, and the women wore rainbows of bright colors. At noon, a wedding took place, and flowers and merriment filled the square.

We were so intrigued by the color and pageantry of Chichicastenango that we stayed longer than we had planned. That evening, we entered into a conversation with several of the native Indians. They were fascinating and very friendly. They told us that the following day they would observe their second Easter, beginning their ceremonies in the morning with hundreds of people singing, then later kneeling and praying in the courtyard in front of the churches.

There was no sense in returning to Guatemala City that evening, so we camped on the outskirts of town.

Although the native Indians were friendly, it was difficult to strike up a conversation with them. They were very reserved and perhaps wary of us. Our appearance surely did not help. We were usually several days between baths and covered with dust. Our clothes, which we often wore several days in a row, were beginning to hang like rags on a beggar. The Indian men were cautious, but once introduced were friendly. They smiled all the time. The women were much less approachable. They were always curious, stealing glances at us out of the corners of their eyes, but when Dave or I looked at them, they would drop their heads or turn their backs.

Returning to Guatemala City that evening, we made some observations about the city traffic. It seemed the farther south we went, the crazier the drivers became.

First, there must have been a zillion motor scooters and small motorcycles in this town. The automobiles, and particularly buses, took the right of way by default, scattering two-wheelers to each side as they plowed down the boulevards. If you happened to be on the curb side, you were liable to be pushed onto the sidewalk.

Second, most drivers at night preferred to drive without head-lights. We never could figure out if it was because the lamps had burned out and were never replaced, or because it was too much trouble to reach over and pull the headlight knob.

Third, the drivers, if they had their lights on, would absolutely not dim them. Not for anyone.

Returning to Guatemala City was a comfortable feeling. We enjoyed the city so much we decided to spend several days tour-ing the city and catching up on our letter-writing.

One afternoon, as we walked leisurely through the downtown area, we heard a commotion coming from around the corner of the next block. It sounded like a large, angry crowd. Hurriedly, we rounded the corner to see what was going on. In our haste, we stumbled directly into the path of a group of students holding anti-U.S. placards. There seemed to be about one hundred of them chanting as they threw rocks at nearby businesses and swung clubs at nothing in particular. A few police stood near the perimeter of the crowd, merely watching.

The crowd was advancing toward us from half a block away. The moment we understood the nature of the mob, they seemed to recognize us as Americans, or at least foreigners, and a few of them began running toward us. Not feeling diplomatic, Dave and I ran back around the corner from where we had come. We man-aged to elude the activists by darting through the El Trebol restau-rant, where we had lunch on occasion.

Guatemala City at night — clean, well-lit boulevards, but little traffic.

We loved this city, but felt it was time to move on. After the incident with the students, small things began to bother us. Even the beautiful waitresses at El Trebol, with whom at first we were infatuated, were beginning to get on our nerves. We talked to everyone we could — politicians, street beggars, shopkeepers, teachers — to get a feel for life in Guatemala.

What we discovered was a beautiful country, rich in history and folklore, yet torn apart by internal strife and political disorder compounded by a strictly divided class system of "haves" and "have-nots." The country had one very valuable man-made resource in the Pan-American Highway. But would the government pave it? Oh no, the politicians managed instead to squander the money on the special interests of the ever-changing players.

We had deliberately not brought weapons with us, reasoning that using them, or even just having them, could create problems. Still, we felt the need for protection and chose to carry a machete, the most inconspicuous weapon. Lots of crazy and violent activities were going on in Central and South America. Tourists were being kidnapped, nuns and priests murdered. Angry demonstrations were commonplace. The militaristic police force was dictatorial, always strutting about with rapid-fire weapons slung over their shoulders. The machete was a tool of life for these people, and it became the same for us. We used it for everything — from cooking to cutting a path through the underbrush in order to set up camp.

On our fiftieth day of the trip, we again hit the road. Leaving Guatemala City we struck out for Antigua, an interesting ruin of a city with a fascinating history.

Three centuries ago, Antigua was the capital of Guatemala. But after being demolished twice by earthquakes and once by a flood, the capital was moved to Guatemala City.

Antigua is beautiful, full of well-preserved ruins and situated midway between two volcanoes that rise to 12,000 feet. We had heard that one of the short-term dictators of Guatemala had planned to improve the country's economy by building a road to the top of one of the volcanoes and establishing a resort there. Thus, he figured, he would attract the rich and famous and use tourist dollars to build the economy.

Good idea, but the most he accomplished was to get a very dusty road carved out of a very steep mountain to about 9,000 feet. The road was so steep that the bikes could not climb the last five hundred feet, so we parked them and hiked to the top.

The view was breathtaking. Huge, billowing cumulus clouds had attached themselves to the mountaintop, and we gazed down through holes in the clouds to the rich, green countryside thousands of feet below. The sight was awe-inspiring, certainly worthy of a mountaintop retreat. Yet we wondered why the dictator did not pave the Pan-American Highway instead of squandering money on this project.

From Antigua, we headed south. The farther we went, the hotter it became, unbearably so in the afternoon. The countryside became savannah-like, an undifferentiated highland, like a humid jungle plain, with innumerable varieties of flying bugs. We crossed into El Salvador.

chapter four
El Salvador

We were beginning to learn the routine of the border stops. Two to three hours of delays while the officials checked, double-checked, and triple-checked passports and visas. Then a superior officer would come out and start the process over again. The strong-arm tactics we encountered upon entering Guatemala proved to be standard at all border crossings.

El Salvador is the smallest Central American country and the most densely populated — about twice the size of New Jersey and three times the population. It also is the only Central American country without a Caribbean coastline.

Up until 1960, El Salvador was considered the least volatile of the Central American republics, but that situation changed abruptly. The economy declined rapidly, due primarily to a drastic drop in the price of the country's two most important crops, coffee and cotton. Accompanying this economic downturn was the beginning of a long period of social and political unrest. El Salvador is a poor country, and the underclass demanded economic and social reforms that were ignored by a succession of military and civilian juntas.

When we arrived in El Salvador, there was little peace in this tiny nation. The tranquility long imposed by the richest citizens was breaking apart at the seams. Ninety percent of the population was a blend of Spanish and Indian, and this populace was becoming agitated.

Unlike the political scenario, the countryside remained peaceful and beautiful. El Salvador is primarily a central plateau lying between two volcanic mountain ranges that run east to west. Many river valleys cut through the plateau, featuring a landscape beautiful and bountiful in its foliage. Being a small country, within a few hours we were in the capital and largest city, San Salvador. Our destination was Lake Ilopango, through the city and somewhat south.

At Chichicastenango, we had met a woman named Gloria who had invited us to stay with her on our way through San Salvador. We threw sleeping bags on her front porch and were serenaded all night by a thunderous tropical rainstorm. We kept thinking it was a good night not to be in the tent.

Gloria was an American who had lived alone in El Salvador most of her fifty-five years. An artist, she relied on the beautiful surroundings to inspire her landscape scenes. Her one-bedroom bungalow sat nestled among the tropical trees on the shore of Lake Ilopango, and her artistic inspirations were obvious.

But Gloria was troubled. She said that the political situation in

Although a small country, El Salvador has its share of beautiful landscapes. Lake Ilopango adds to the beauty of the countryside.

El Salvador was creating such discontent that at times she did not feel safe in her own home. Several murders had recently occurred nearby, and she was considering returning to the United States. It was a sad commentary coming from such a wonderful person.

Although our stay in El Salvador was short, we have pleasant memories, thanks to Gloria's hospitality. After a swim in the lake and a big breakfast, we climbed on the bikes, determined to make up some of the time we had lost in Guatemala.

The rainstorm passed, and it became stifling hot. We tried riding without shirts, but the sun was too strong. So once again we tried to dress coolly, yet protected, and smeared white cream all over our faces.

chapter five

Honduras

After the customary border hassles, we crossed into Honduras. The Pan-American Highway cut across the southwestern end of Honduras, skirting the Golfo de Fonseca.

Although Honduras is a large country by Central American standards (roughly the size of Pennsylvania), the highway crosses through the southern tip for only one hundred miles.

The heat was overpowering. We understood why the afternoon siesta was commonplace. It was simply too hot to do anything productive. Even the evenings were hot. We were now in the habit of laying the tent down like a ground cover, spreading the sleeping bags on top, and lying on top of the bags.

Dust also was a problem. Since leaving Mexico, most of the Pan-American Highway had been nothing more than a dirt road and often not a very good one. We could not travel side by side, because avoiding chuckholes, rocks, chickens, and other assorted obstacles required maneuverability. So we traveled about five minutes apart, in one-hour segments. On the hour, the lead bike would stop and wait for the trailing rider. We would compare notes of things we had seen and pictures we had taken.

We would then reverse positions, the trailing rider now becoming the lead rider. This enabled each of us to have about a fifteen-minute break every other hour, five minutes waiting for the trailing rider, five minutes talking, and five minutes allowing the new lead rider to get a head start. The main reason for this system, however, was to let the dust settle. That five-minute interval, even with the lead rider stopping for pictures, allowed us both to have a clear road.

Honduras has many similarities with its neighbor, El Salvador. Its political history is also rampant with military coups, dictators, and presidents succeeding one another with alarming rapidity. It relies on coffee as well as bananas and even a little silver and gold to support the economy. But even with these riches, Honduras, like El Salvador, remained mired in nagging poverty. One foreign economist described the situation in 1963 as "a frightening and frustrating economy."

Unlike El Salvador, Honduras is sparsely populated. The population is primarily mestizo (Spanish and Indian ancestry) but the concentrations of inhabitants are located in small villages in the north coastal and central areas.

Due to our short ride through the southern tip of the country, our exposure to Hondurans was limited to a few people who lived in extreme poverty. As we had previously experienced, these people were wary of us, but once a proper introduction had been made they were warm and friendly.

chapter six

Nicaragua

Crossing into Nicaragua was easy, with a new customs building and a fairly well-organized system. We should have known there would be a catch. Fifteen miles took us to Somotillo where a roadside customs official told us we were required to report to the main customs station in Managua.

This portion of Nicaragua was similar to Honduras — desert-like and hot. Though we tried to avoid each other's dust trail, occasionally we would catch some of our own dust or that of another passing vehicle. The heat made us break out in a sweat, and the dust clung to our bodies like a second layer of skin. We seldom enjoyed the luxury of a shower, but every time we crossed a stream we would jump in, clothes and all.

Nicaragua is the largest of the Central American republics, roughly the size of Michigan. It is triangular in shape, and the Pan-American Highway runs for about 250 miles along the Pacific Ocean side of the triangle. For more than one hundred miles, the highway skirts the shores of Lake Managua and Lake Nicaragua, the largest lake in Central America.

Because of these lakes and the configuration of the country and its terrain, Nicaragua had, in the early part of the twentieth century, the ill luck to be considered as the most likely spot for a trans-isthmian canal, linking the Pacific and the Atlantic. Some discussion even involved a sea-level canal. All this attention to Nicaragua attracted the ambitions of the great powers of the world. The ensuing years saw Nicaragua suffer a tortuous course of instability. Partially as a result, Nicaragua remains largely undeveloped, even though it is rich in natural resources.

We arrived in Managua at 2 p.m. and reported to the necessary customs station only to discover a sign on the door saying that it had closed at 1 p.m. and would not open until 8 a.m. the following day. Par for the course.

Once again, we had to stay in the city, so we sought a cheap room. Similar to the others in which we had stayed, the room was ten feet on a side with a wood floor, divided in half with a wood partition that nearly reached the ceiling. A bulb with no shade hung from a dangling electrical cord to just about head height. The walls at one time had been painted but now had discolored and faded to an obscure beige, stained from floor to ceiling with blotches of different colors and consistency.

The bugs didn't mind, though. An assortment of crawling and flying varmints graciously shared these accommodations with us. We had a little of everything — cockroaches, flies, spiders, and a variety of flying insects both large and small.

We had grown accustomed to living with these creatures, but

this spot was particularly infested, and it bothered us because we knew that until recently the region had been ravaged by yellow fever and malaria.

Many proprietors of the hotels in which we stayed raised their own chickens, pigs, and other barnyard animals that would both keep us awake throughout the night and make sure we were up at sunrise. Additionally, people talked and generally functioned all night long, sleeping during the hot, daylight hours. We always looked forward to leaving the cities and heading into the country-side to get some peace and quiet.

The immigration office was packed at 8 a.m., with people forming a long line out the door. We had expected this and arrived early. After shuffling between counters for several hours, we learned we could cross the border on Saturday. It was now only Wednesday. But we took a chance and headed for the Costa Rican border anyway. The trip around Lake Nicaragua was pleasant, the weather good, though hot.

We were lucky. We struck up a friendly conversation with the border guard, and he allowed us to cross, saving us three days of idleness.

chapter seven
Costa Rica

We set camp in early evening our first night in Costa Rica. Once again, we found a dry creek bed and traveled about one quarter-mile up the dry wash to establish camp. On the way up the arroyo, about one hundred yards off the highway, we passed a huge, dead iguana. We stopped and inspected him to make sure he was dead. He measured more than five feet from nose to tail. Reassured that he was dead, we traveled another several hundred yards to set our campsite.

The next morning, as we followed our tracks back to the highway, we came to the spot where the iguana had been the evening before. He was gone. We were sure of the spot, because we saw our tire tracks and footprints from the previous evening.

Upon further examination, we found the last two inches of his tail lying in the sand. No other tracks were apparent. We deduced that an army of ants must have carved up and hauled off the carcass overnight. Thinking about our camp just up the creekbed from this incident was unsettling.

We got an early start the next morning. We wanted to get to San José for we had heard what a beautiful city it was, including the people. We planned to stay a few days, finding out for ourselves. San José is the capital of Costa Rica and sits in the center of the country, an easy day's drive to either border under normal conditions.

We started that morning under clear skies and warm weather. But everything turned for the worse. The map did not indicate the deplorable condition of the road, and we began to wonder if reaching San José by nightfall was possible. Then the road really began to deteriorate. At times, it was like driving through a narrow rock quarry, with loose rocks making up the roadbed. The tires on the bikes would roll off the sides of the rocks, bouncing the machines from one rock to another.

Then the wind picked up. Off in the distance, we could see a huge black cloud that appeared to mushroom from the ground up. As we got closer, it spread in size, blown by the wind. We both thought that it was a forest fire, but if so it was a big one.

Dave and I traded the lead two more times, all the time keeping an eye on the cloud. The going was slow because of the rock path commonly known as the Pan-American Highway, but we were definitely driving straight toward the cloud. About an hour outside of San José, I caught up with Dave to change leads. We took off our helmets to talk, and stared at each other. Our faces were black, covered with soot, dust, and grime. We realized that we had actually entered the cloud.

Mount Irazú is a short distance east of San José, rising to over 11,000 feet in elevation. We understood that from its peak, on a

When we found a clean stream, we often tended to loiter. Dave does his weekly wash.

clear day, both the Atlantic and the Pacific oceans are visible. But not today. For eight days, volcanic ash had been billowing into the atmosphere.

As we neared San José, ash was everywhere. Our bikes created both a rooster tail and a wake as we drove down the streets. The stuff was packed up against the curbs and doorways.

The city had an eerie appearance, with the dull, dark gray ash clinging to everything. There was little movement in the streets, but when people did step outside they were fully covered, including their faces, so they would not breathe the ash. Dave and I had taken to covering our faces as well. Even so, it was hard to breathe. After traveling for an hour, our ears were caked (despite wearing our helmets), and we had to clean them out to hear each other.

Dusk was approaching and we decided to take a room for the

night. Under the circumstances, we thought we deserved a little better than the rundown hotels in which we usually stayed. Afterward, we were not sure it was worth the extra money because the ash had infiltrated the room, seeping in around the window frames. The room was covered with a fine layer of dust. Additionally, the city fathers had asked that water be used very sparingly, for they did not know how long this situation would last, and the reservoir had been contaminated with the ash.

So our stay in San José was short. We left early the next morning. Just south of the city, we emerged from the cloud of ash. We were concerned about the ash's effect on the engines, so we stopped and cleaned the carburetors and other essential parts that we could reach.

Leaving San José, the road was paved and we thought we would finally be able to make good time. Cordoba, a short fourteen miles from San Jose, was the extent of our luck. Here, the highway turned from good to bad to awful. We traveled for ten hours and covered slightly over one hundred miles.

The road began to climb up the Cordillera de Talmanca, and ahead lay the highest passes and some of the steepest grades in Central America. The highway was full of rocks, boulders, chuckholes, deep gravel, and small ravines where water had run off across the road and sometimes straight down the middle. The sky was overcast, and we could see that the road led directly into the clouds.

About halfway up the grade, we entered fog. Water was running down the road, so we donned our raingear, expecting the weather to get worse. It did. The temperature was still warm, and

Much of the time, the Pan-American Highway more closely resembled a riverbed than a highway, greatly inhibiting commerce.

the fog seemed to cling to us, misting and steaming our glasses. Soon, it was difficult to see where we were going. As we climbed the grade, the weather got wetter, and soon we were pushing through a driving rainstorm.

The rain was not what bothered us, though; it was the mud. The dirt road had more water than it could handle and was turning into a muddy creek, with more muddy water slowly sliding down the mountain. Because of the mud and the difficulty we had seeing through the rain, we occasionally hit one of the rocks or chuckholes in the road. On a few occasions, we even lost balance and laid the bikes over in the mud.

At the summit (11,500 feet in elevation) was a small restaurant. Although early afternoon, it was not open, but we pounded on the door until someone came. We were determined to get warm and dry. The owner was very pleasant. He had closed for the day thinking that no one would be able to climb the grade in that weather.

He fixed us a cup of coffee, and we sat and talked with him in Spanish as we dried out. After half an hour, we felt the need to get moving. We put on our raingear, stepped outside, and headed toward the bikes. In the distance, we heard a familiar sound — like motorcycle engines climbing a steep grade. Moments later, two riders appeared out of the mist. Dave and I naturally wanted to find out who they were, so we re-entered the restaurant with them.

John and Bill were two brothers who both lived in California, but in different cities. Like Dave and me, they thought it would be adventurous to travel through Central America on motorcycles. Both in their mid to late twenties, they had taken several months off from their jobs and headed south. Bill was on a new Honda 305 and John was on a Harley-Davidson 650.

They had not done the research we had and were surprised by the difficulty of the trip. Their intention was to travel to Panama City and then double back to California.

Not realizing how long the trip would take and being behind schedule, they had been traveling as quickly as possible, with few detours for sightseeing or city experiences. They knew about us, because they had been following in our tracks, expecting to catch up with us at some point. They admitted, though, that they had not thought it would happen in this unlikely spot. We hit it off and decided to travel as a group from that point on.

We bounced along the top of the Cordillera for a few miles and then started the descent. As we dropped off the mountain range, the weather improved dramatically, but the road did not. In fact, the road deteriorated even more. With only two wheels under us, getting down the mountain was tough.

We set camp and rose the next morning with the sun. What a difference a day could make. By midmorning, it was hot and turning sultry.

We stopped at a roadside cafe for a Coca-Cola and happened to meet a fellow named Jerry Weber. Jerry had been born in the United States, but when he was a teenager his father bought a plantation and moved the family to Costa Rica. He offered to give us a tour, and we gladly accepted.

This was not a plantation like you may have seen in the movies about the Old South. The house was small, especially for four people. It was built of stucco with a tile roof and had obviously been there for a long time. Jerry pointed out that the house leaned a little bit to the starboard, as it had since he and his brother had bought it from their father thirteen years before. Four wooden steps led up to a wooden front porch that tilted away from the front of the house. There was no indoor plumbing or air conditioning and the house was warm. But of course, it was about 100 degrees outside.

What was impressive, however, was the crop: coffee, cocoa, grapefruit, rubber, oranges, bananas, and a few other fruits. Jerry spent the better part of the morning showing us the operation and how he and his brother worked the crops.

Their property covered about a hundred acres, and the two brothers primarily worked the crops themselves. As a particular fruit came into season, they would hire locals to help harvest the

A plantation house in Costa Rica.

crop. The crops were then handled by intermediaries who would sell the product to one of the large consortiums that controlled the various markets.

We asked if they returned to the states often, and Jerry replied that it had been eight years since his last visit. This was his home, and except for occasional vacations (which he indicated were few and far between), there was nothing for him in the states.

Back on the highway in the afternoon, we were tiring of fighting the road. Conditions had not improved and were similar to driving along the bottom of a swift creek, without the water. The road made a long, sweeping left turn, and we could see the rocks and boulders begging us to take them on. Three of us did.

John, however, spotted a trail through a field which appeared to cut across the crescent of the turn. He headed his Harley onto the path, and we saw his handlebars and upper body racing across the field. We envied his ingenuity. We were slowly bumping down the road while he was flying along. All three of us were watching him when suddenly he disappeared.

He reappeared a moment later, and we could tell he was in trouble. He was well off the seat of the bike and trying desperately to hold on to the handlebars. The entire bike came into view, and it was obvious he had catapulted off a jump of some sort. Once again, he disappeared from view, reappearing moments later. But this time, he was free of the bike and somersaulting through the air. The bike was adjacent to him but flying freely in another direction.

The three of us immediately cut through the field and found John off to the side of the path, moaning and holding his leg. The bike was lying on its side, sputtering, on the opposite side of the path. After assessing the situation, we found the bike to be bent, but ridable, and John's ego to be hurt more than anything else, although he was sore for several days.

We took our time getting to the Panamanian border. John and Bill had decided to forget about hurrying, willing to suffer the consequences. The weather was hot, and since many streams were in the area, we spent several hours each day swimming. We were having a good time getting to know these guys, yet we were not close enough to them for there to be any friction.

We talked about it one night and found that they concurred with us about traveling by motorcycle. You are left to your own thoughts most of the day and do not have a chance to irritate your partner, at least while riding. We had originally considered making this trip by Jeep or Land Rover, but figured that we would drive each other crazy spending all day, every day, sitting side by side.

chapter eight

Panama

Our last night in Costa Rica was most enjoyable as we camped once again along the side of a creek. John was quite sore from his acrobatics earlier in the day, and we knew several days would pass before he returned to his normal physical condition.

Because of this, we got a late start the next morning. Although the border was only fifty miles away, the road was so terrible that the ride took several hours. Shortly after noon, we arrived at the Panamanian border. Because it was lunchtime, we had to wait an additional hour for the border guards to return to their posts. Then we lost yet another hour, for as we passed into Panama we crossed into the Eastern Standard time zone. We were now due south of Florida.

We had been two months on the road. At times, we had difficulty referring to it as a road. It was more like a cow path. However, we had heard that a new highway was being built in Panama, so we were expecting driving conditions to improve. And they did, for the most part.

Panama was in the process of building a new concrete highway from the Costa Rican border to Panama City. The government was serious enough about it to get the United States to help build it. The construction crew consisted of Panamanian workers with American supervision, technology, and equipment. This substantial foreign aid was providing an excellent highway.

We discovered how badly the new highway was needed when we had to detour around an unfinished portion. These sections were miserable — the worst driving conditions we had seen. Usually fifteen to twenty miles in length, these detours were extremely slow, with potholes, deep gravel, and even streams that had to be forded.

On a couple of occasions in Costa Rica, we had to cross streams because bridges were not built, but here in Panama, we had to drive right through a few shallow rivers. After crossing the border, we anticipated three days of driving to get to Panama City, even with the slow detours.

The four of us were taking our time and enjoying the countryside. We had expected jungle in Panama, but so far the country was flat and prairie-like. A broadleaf grass grew about three feet high and extended endlessly, surrounding trees and rocks and creating a beautiful carpet over the countryside. The grass was bright green, as rain fell for a brief period every afternoon, and it swayed like a hula skirt in the breeze. The weather was hot, but a slight breeze picked up in the afternoon, providing relief from the temperature as well as helping to eliminate bug problems while driving.

We had been sleeping in the tent and cooking our own meals for quite some time and knew that in Panama City we would be packing our gear and adapting to a more urbane lifestyle, including hotels. Therefore, we had some major feasts along the roadside, trying to use up our food supply. Breakfast started early, around 6:30 a.m., and consisted of juice, hot chocolate, eggs, hotcakes, toast, honey, peanut butter, and occasionally anything else we could scrape together, such as cheese or soup. After a breakfast like that, lunch was normally a Coca-Cola and a hastily prepared sandwich. For dinner, we would buy a chicken or pick up some canned food at one of the local markets.

Three days later, we arrived in Panama City. Since the four of us would be staying a few days, we decided to get one room that would accommodate us all. We found a sleazy little hotel about six blocks from the center of town where we rented a room for seventy-five cents apiece. It was a fairly small rectangular space with four cots arranged in the center. The space was so tight that it was difficult to stand between the cots or to walk about, but it served our purpose. A fan hung from the ceiling in the center of the room, and a double door opened onto a narrow balcony. Both were appreciated because of the heat.

We would be in Panama for several days while we prepared for our push into South America. For that time, we called this room home. Once again, we shared a communal bathroom with everyone else on the floor, and although at times inconvenient, we were now growing used to it. There was one small closet in the room, but it really did not matter because we had little to hang. All our clothes had been packed in the saddle boxes, and John and Bill had merely strapped suitcases to the backs of their rigs. Most of the clothes were brought up to the room. Consequently, we had stuff scattered everywhere on the floor. The easiest way to get from the door to the balcony was to walk across the four cots. This did not present a problem, unless someone had to get up in the middle of the night.

Just after renting the room, we went to the local market and shopped for fresh fruit. The supply was abundant — an assortment of oranges, papayas, plantains, and other tropical fruit. We bought a stalk of bananas and, back in our room, hung it on the door knobs of the double doors to the balcony. The fruit served two purposes. First it was good for snacking, and second, it attracted lots of flies which therefore left us alone.

As the days passed, we began to get familiar with Panama City. It was a delight, an industrious city with a friendly population. The canal was built and still partially managed by the United States. Military bases established to protect the canal meant lots of Americans lived throughout the region. Hence, we were in daily contact with English-speaking people.

Our first full day in the city was spent just driving around to get a feeling for the town. The four of us decided to visit the canal about noon with nothing more in mind than driving along it for a distance. When we arrived, however, we noted a sign indicating that the Miraflores locks (those on the Pacific side) were open to the public for viewing. We parked the four bikes next to the entrance gate and entered the canal grounds. As we waited a few minutes for the next tour to start, we heard a broadcast over the intercom system that startled us.

"Will the individuals owning the motorcycles parked at the

main gate please report to the control tower office immediately."
We glanced at each other, wondering what we had done wrong
this time.

We knocked on the door to the control tower office, and the
door opened immediately. Standing in front of us was a large,
heavy-framed man wearing a hard hat with the word "Lockmaster"
stenciled across its front. Holding out his hand for introduction, he
said, "Hi, my name is Joe Young, and I am the lockmaster for the
Miraflores portion of the canal. One of the employees here noticed your bikes parked at the front gate and mentioned them to
me. I am a motorcycle fanatic, and so I went out to see for myself.
When I noticed the Oregon and California license plates, I knew I
had to meet the guys who owned them."

We responded in turn, and Joe invited us into his office. Our
first comments were salutatory in nature. Some general discussion followed regarding why we were making the trip, the length
of time we had been on the road, how we had caught up with
one another, and so forth. The more we talked, the more intrigued
Joe became with our odyssey, and we settled into a general account of the journey's events to date. He interrupted frequently
with questions, and we could tell our story fascinated him. Realizing he was supposed to be working, we suggested we get together later and continue the conversation, to which Joe enthusi-
astically agreed.

We planned to return to the lobby to join the small group
forming for the next tour, but Joe would not hear of it. He insisted
on personally guiding us on an extensive tour of the locks. He
mentioned that because of repair work being done, he needed to

make an inspection tour himself, and we would not be inconveniencing him.

Before starting the tour, Joe gave us an introduction to the canal and its history.

"Prior to the turn of the twentieth century, there had been considerable discussion regarding a canal linking the Pacific and Atlantic oceans. Construction of such a canal would eliminate the need to round the tip of South America through the treacherous Strait of Magellan. The building of such a canal would save several weeks additional sailing," he explained.

"At first, it was thought a sea-level canal could be built, but in 1905 the Isthmian Canal Commission decided to build a canal with locks instead. The Panamanian government had granted a strip of land to the United States in 1903 for the purpose of construction, operation, maintenance, and protection of the Panama Canal. Originally, the U.S. was to operate the canal in perpetuity, but in later years the original treaties were repealed and new ones written which will turn control of the canal over to Panama by the year 2000."

He continued, "The actual building of the canal, with all of its construction problems and political unrest at the time, is a fascinating story in itself and ranks as one of the greatest engineering works of all time. We'll skip that part of the story and suffice it to say that the canal was finished on schedule and first opened for limited use in 1914.

"The canal is about forty miles in length, not including the dredged approach channels, and at its minimum width is the length of a football field. The approach from the Atlantic proceeds inland

The Panama Canal is drained once every five years for cleaning. We were fortunate to be there during the two-week cleaning cycle.

at sea level for about eleven miles to the Gatún Locks. Through a series of three locks, ships are lifted eighty-five feet to the level of Lake Gatún, which was formed by damming the Chagres River. Ships pass through the lake and exit through the Gaillard Cut, which is an excavated channel about eight miles long. At the end of the Gaillard Cut are the Pedro Miguel locks, which drop the ships thirty-one feet and into Lake Miraflores. The ships pass through the lake and then drop to sea level through the two Miraflores locks at the Pacific end of the canal.

"It sounds rather simple," Joe said, "but of course there are auxiliary facilities which also had to be constructed to control the canal. Other dams and reservoirs had to be built to maintain constant levels in the Gatún and Miraflores lakes, as well as breakwaters and hydroelectric plants to generate power and the Panama

Railway which carries supplies.

"The important thing for you today, however," he continued, "is that the canal was constructed with a double parallel set of locks so that one ship can be lifted while another is being lowered. Once every five years, we drain each side of the canal for a two-week period to do preventive maintenance and cleaning. You just happen to be here during that time. Once we get clearance from the tower, we will be able to walk down onto the floor of the locks, and I'll show you how it all works."

We continued to descend the control tower and stepped out onto the concrete surface of the Miraflores locks. The lock to our right had a large freighter in it, which was being towed by lines running from the bow of the ship to one of the locomotives that operate as "tuggers" along the surface of the lock. The lock to our left was dry. Peering down, we could see a number of workmen moving about on the floor of the lock.

"We are going to step down onto the floor of the lock with those workmen," Joe said. "A lot of welding is going on down there, and cranes are lifting and lowering equipment, so walk carefully and make sure you keep your hard hat on."

We descended via scaffolding and stairways into the lock. All the while, Joe continued to comment on details of the locks. He explained in great detail the inner workings of the locks — how the water is transferred in and out of the chambers through tunnels and piping, how the gates of each lock work, and so on. We were amazed by the condition of the locks after fifty years of service. They looked like new and had been maintained expertly so that they operated as well as they had the day the canal opened. Joe mentioned that few visitors are ever allowed such a close inspection of the canal, and we were both appreciative and fascinated.

Three hours later, we returned to the control tower and agreed to get together soon to talk about our adventures.

The four of us, but particularly Dave and me, struck up a close friendship with Joe Young, even though he was twenty years our senior. He was a likable, easygoing guy. At first look, he seemed rough and tough, but this was because of his six-foot-four-inch, 250-pound frame. His appearance was deceiving, for he was actually more like a teddy bear. There are some people in this world who are just plain "nice guys," and Joe was one of them. As we got to know Joe, we found him to be sincere, honest, and a good friend. He was one of those people who would do anything possible to help someone he was close to.

After our chance meeting at the locks, we began to spend time with Joe and his wife, Connie. Like Joe, Connie enjoyed motorcycling, and they belonged to a local club. They were both interested in our exploits and liked to sit around in the evening swapping stories. One evening, they invited all their motorcycling friends over to hear about our experience. As the guests arrived that evening, we noticed that they did not look like a motorcycle group. They were mostly middle-aged and appeared fairly well-to-do.

In fact, John, Bill, Dave, and I were the ones who looked out of place. Each of us had been carrying one pair of slacks and a sportcoat, but they had been packed away in the boxes so long that they were unwearable. Therefore, we donned our regular attire of jeans and long-sleeved plaid shirts. We did, however, change our boots in favor of casual dress shoes.

Furthermore, Dave and I had continued to let our beards grow. Mine had blossomed into a fairly thick growth, but it was bright red and the rest of my hair is brown, so it looked a little weird. But Dave was another story. For some reason, he had let his small patches of beard grow to several inches in length.

The guests did not seem to mind our appearances, for we had a pleasant evening sharing experiences. These people were also a big help in terms of giving us good advice about fixing some minor problems with the bikes. We knew we would be staying in Panama City for several days and needed some repairs to the cycles, and they steered us to some specialists who got the job done right.

Other than the minor repairs, the BMWs were holding up well. We had traveled approximately 10,000 miles in three months. Other than Dave's crash in Mexico and my clutch problem in Guatemala, we had enjoyed relatively trouble-free performance. We had suffered two flat tires, occasional dust in the carburetors and air filters, and a few minor adjustments. But other than that, the motorcycles had performed beyond our expectations.

Our days in Panama City were fun. We would leave our little hotel room by midmorning and drive off in a different direction each day, exploring first the town and then the countryside.

One day, we followed the canal a short way up to Madden Dam, one of the auxiliary facilities for controlling the canal. On the return trip, we passed through a tropical forest reserve and witnessed an incredible ant colony.

These ants were huge, about an inch in length. Tens of thousands of them formed two parallel columns traveling in opposite directions. The ants headed in one direction were carrying leaves or parts of leaves, which other ants had chewed into portable sections. They were depositing these leaf sections into a huge pile, creating a hill of material. The hill was about six feet high and ten feet in diameter. Another group of ants was roaming on the hill itself, strategically placing the leaf sections on the mound. The transporting ants would then return to the jungle to haul more leaves. The ants had cut a swath about twenty feet wide through the foliage, and for about two hundred feet, the jungle was stripped bare.

It was amazing to watch. We marveled at the genius of nature and how a process like this could carry on. It was also a little scary, for it reminded us of the iguana in Costa Rica that had mysteriously disappeared overnight. Was it a process like this that devoured that carcass?

The Pan-American Highway is a system of highways extending from Alaska through South America. The northern section of the route begins in Fairbanks, Alaska, and extends through British Columbia to the Canada-U.S. border.

In the United States, the highway becomes Interstate 5 through Washington, Oregon, and California to the U.S.-Mexico border. In Mexico and Central America, the road is called the Inter-American Highway. Several spokes of the highway reach from the U.S.-Mexico border to Mexico City. From Mexico City to Panama City, the highway becomes the single roadway that we had just traveled.

In South America, the highway follows the continent's west coast to Santiago, Chile, turning east across the Andes mountains to Buenos Aires, Argentina. Here, the highway branches out to the other countries along the continent's east coast.

The first Pan-American Highway Congress was held in Buenos Aires in 1925, and the goal of the North and South American countries in attendance was to provide an international highway system spider-webbing the continents. By 1963, some progress had been made, but the route we had traveled the last few months could hardly be classified as a highway. What we did not know was that the worst was yet to come.

In one form or another, however, the highway did extend uninterrupted from Alaska through Chile, with one exception.

Somewhat south of Panama City, the jungle begins and extends approximately one hundred miles to Barranquilla in northwest Colombia. This stretch of jungle through the southern portion of the Isthmus of Panama is known as the Darién Gap. Some people claim this to be the densest jungle in the world. There are no established roads through this section, and it is nearly impenetrable by vehicle.

We knew that we would have to ship the bikes to South America in order to continue our journey, but we wanted to get a look at this jungle impeding our overland travel. Therefore, on one of our side excursions, we traveled south of Panama City to find the end of the highway in Central America.

A few miles out of town, the road deteriorated. Little traveled, it turned into a dirt road that bounced over the countryside and, devoid of bridges, sloshed through several creeks and rivers. About twenty miles south of Panama City, the road ended abruptly.

The drive south of Panama City passed through typical Panamanian countryside, with a few farmers trying desperately to make a living out of the tropical savannah. But at this point, the road ran head on into the beginning of the Darién Gap. The jungle was like a wall extending across the land. There was no lead-up to it. All of a sudden, it emerged from the surrounding, flat countryside.

We drove up to the jungle wall and parked the bikes. Stepping into the underbrush made it clear why no road had been carved through it. Towering trees and plants were intertwined with vines, making even walking very difficult.

I stood outside the wall while Dave stepped into the jungle. About twenty feet into the undergrowth, he was gone. I could hear him but not see him, and we now understood why it would be necessary to take a sea route into South America.

Returning to Panama City, we were overtaken by a motorcycle policeman riding an old Harley-Davidson "hog" with a side-mounted hand shifter. His motorcycle had seen lots of miles, for it was dinged and dented all over, but he was obviously very proud of it because it was polished to a bright silver shine. He motioned us to the side of the road and, complying, we parked and dismounted the bikes. We felt this might be a curiosity stop since we did not believe we had done anything legally wrong.

He put his kickstand down, stepped off his machine, and approached us. Fully dressed out in his Panamanian police uniform, we were impressed with his official appearance. He looked like a figure of authority. Furthermore, we were surprised by the size of this man. Panamanians usually are not large people, but this guy was. He was not only quite tall, but heavyset as well. With his pistol, billy club, and full ring of keys dangling at his side, he looked like the sort of person we would want as a friend, not an enemy.

He marched directly up to us, and as he began to speak, we were aware of his glistening white teeth contrasted against his dark skin. His smile put us at immediate ease. He introduced himself as Baltimore and spoke in Caribbean-accented English. We obviously looked out of place in this part of the country, and he was checking as to our purpose. Noticing our Oregon license plates, he was further curious and apparently just wanted to question us in general.

His first questions were obvious ones: how far had we come, where were we going, etc. As we developed a dialogue with Baltimore, we found him to be an intelligent person, and we asked about his background.

He told us, "I was born in Panama, but at an early age my father moved the family to Jamaica. He worked in Panama City for a cruise line, and they wanted him to work out of the Jamaica office for a few years. During those early years in Jamaica, I learned English. My father had to have a good working vocabulary in English for his office job with the cruise line, and so he would come home and use English around the house all the time. My mother couldn't understand a word he was saying, but I picked it up in a hurry. Besides, I was about eight years old then, and they were using English in the school I attended.

"I am the oldest of six kids in the family, and soon we had the whole tribe speaking English, except for my mom, of course. She had some sort of fundamental resistance toward even trying to speak the language. Then when we moved back to Panama, I had lots of opportunities to continue using my English, with all of the canal workers and military in the area. Now that I am in the police force, I am stationed near the Canal Zone so I can interact with the English-speaking authorities."

We asked, "What are you doing out of the city in uniform? It seems odd that you would travel down here on this dusty dirt road while you are on duty."

"I live down here," he replied. "My wife and nine children live just around that bend in the road. You just passed it. I am off duty now and on my way home. I would be honored if you would come to my home and meet my family."

We accepted Baltimore's invitation, although we felt a little reluctant to go barging into his home.

We had not noticed his house the first time we passed, although it was visible from the road. It sat back from the dirt highway a couple of hundred feet and was situated on a gently rising knoll, perhaps twenty feet above the level of the road. A single-lane dirt path led from the road to the house. Heavy growth bordered each side of the narrow path. The only traffic on the path was Baltimore's motorcycle or his wife or kids walking from the house to the road.

We drove up to the house and were greeted by about twenty kids, yelling and screaming and jumping up and down. Baltimore quieted them and introduced six of his children, ranging in age from three to ten. The rest of the kids, he explained, were neighbors, although as we looked around the surrounding area, we could not see any other dwellings.

As we dismounted the bikes, Baltimore's wife emerged from the house. She was in the process of breast-feeding a baby and had two toddlers in tow, both of them holding onto the bottom of her skirt. She, like Baltimore, was heavyset and probably in her mid thirties, although she looked closer to fifty.

The life that these people live is demanding and difficult, particularly for those who live outside the city and do not belong to the privileged class. These families usually have many children, often one each year. Not only is it considered proof of a man's masculinity to sire many children, but a large family is needed to help with farming chores.

Baltimore and his wife were lucky. They had lost only one of their children to disease. But Baltimore was quick to point out that he was well-read, believed in doctors, and earned a good income with which to support his family. Most people in rural areas of Latin America were not so fortunate.

Baltimore introduced Dave and me to his wife, who continued to feed the baby through the introduction, and invited us inside. He had to get a little stern with the kids outside, because they all wanted to come in also and listen to the conversation. They did not realize they would not be able to understand the language.

Baltimore's house was typical of the area. A square structure about thirty feet on each side, the walls were constructed primarily of spindly trees and stalks of sugar cane. Bamboo might be used if available, but was not in this house. A crude type of mud stucco was plastered between the cane and tree trunks on the outside of the house. The roof was thatch, and although not

Baltimore, a Panamanian policeman, his family, and two friends gather for their first family portrait. They stand in front of their home a few miles south of Panama City.

particularly thick, had been woven tightly to keep the rain out.

Inside the house was one large room, with narrow-cane movable screens separating major living areas. Baltimore and his wife shared one divided area. Most of the kids, except for the babies, had cots lined up in a tight row against one wall. We suggested to Baltimore that he might stack the cots like bunk beds along the wall to create more space. He said that was a great idea and wondered why he hadn't thought of it.

A few chairs and mats were spread around the main living area, and a few pieces of furniture stored clothes. Colorful woven rugs hung on the inside walls, and although there was no electricity for light, the wall hangings brightened the room.

Two essential rooms were located outside the main building. The bathroom was an outhouse situated some distance behind the house, a well-worn path leading to it. The kitchen was immediately to the side and toward the back of the house. A door opened directly from the house into the yard in front of the kitchen. The kitchen was a freestanding lean-to kind of structure with cane walls. On two sides, the individual canes were spaced apart so that the smoke could escape. The back wall of the kitchen was also cane, but closely tied to keep the wind from whipping through. The roof consisted of odd-sized pieces of corrugated metal held in place by loose thatch. The front of the structure was open so that food could easily be carried from the kitchen directly into the house. Baltimore had managed to find an old wood-burning stove, and the family used this for cooking. "A big improvement over the open fire that most have to deal with," he said.

Baltimore's house differed from most of the others throughout the countryside in that his had a floor. He had been able to buy sheets of plywood, which he had then secured to a wooden foundation. Woven rugs covered the plywood. Baltimore was very proud of his home, but he talked most about the floor. He would grin widely and his teeth would flash through his dark complexion as he talked about his floor.

We spent several hours talking with Baltimore, mostly about our escapades and his life as a policeman. As dusk began to settle, we felt we should be going. Baltimore insisted that we stay for dinner, but after seeing the kitchen and remembering the queasy stomachs we had been experiencing lately, we declined. After thanking Baltimore profusely for his hospitality, we drove back to Panama City.

We arrived back at the room well after dark to find John and

Bill packing their things. They were going to pull out first thing in the morning for their return trip to California and wanted to be ready for an early start. They had been telling us over the last several days that they needed to get back to work but until then they had not seemed to be in any hurry. It had taken Dave and me several months to get that far, and now they were hoping to return in two weeks. They probably could. There was only one road, and they were now familiar with it. By putting in long days in the saddle, they should be able to keep their timetable, but the trip wouldn't be much fun.

We said our goodbyes that night, for they intended to leave at dawn. We had enjoyed the company of John and Bill because they broke up the monotony that Dave and I had begun to experience with one another. However, we were ready to settle back into the routine of just the two of us. Furthermore, they had considerably more money to spend than we did, and we felt awkward about our frugality. At times, it led to disputes about where to eat, for example. They often went to a restaurant, while we ate fruit in the room. The time was right, we felt, to part company.

We awoke to find that John and Bill had departed, and now the time had arrived for us to get on with our travels. The first order of business was to arrange passage into South America. Over the last several days, we had checked with the local authorities to ensure that our papers were in order. Now we needed to figure out how we would get there.

Our first stop was to see Joe Young. He informed us that, in order to maintain an even flow of traffic, ships passed through the canal berth at the entrance to the passage, not on the exiting end. Therefore, if we headed to Venezuela, we would need to board at Balboa on the Pacific side; if we headed to Colombia, we would need to drive to Colón on the Atlantic side and board there. Either way, we were looking at passage through the canal on a ship, an unexpected pleasure.

We first tried to book passage to Venezuela, but because of the repair work being performed to the locks on the Pacific side, the ships were stacked up several deep waiting to get to the dock prior to entering the canal. It took us one full day to determine that none of the ships currently in port would be able to accommodate us. They could take the bikes, but they did not have room for us as passengers.

We could have shipped the bikes and then flown to meet them, but we were reluctant to do that. First, we did not feel comfortable leaving the machines at the mercy of the Panamanian and Venezuelan longshoremen. Secondly, we did not have enough money to fly to South America.

The following day, we made the hour-and-a-half trip to Colón, the port city on the Atlantic side of the canal. First, we visited the shipping agents in an attempt to book passage, but they were no help at all. They were interested in large cargo and did not want to be bothered with a couple of Americans trying to get their motor-cycles into South America.

So we set out on our own and toured the piers looking for a ship that would take us to Colombia. We went to the yacht club to see if we could get some leads, but to no avail. We then went to Folk's River, which is the poorest section of Colón, looking for a banana boat that would book us passage. Eventually, we ended up at Pier 3 where we learned that two ships heading for Colombia would be arriving the following day.

We returned to Panama City, and realizing that Joe Young would be home from work, decided to stop by his house. He was glad to see us, and after some brief conversation, told us that he wanted to show us something in town. The three of us piled into his Fiat 600 and headed for downtown Panama City. Joe lived in the Canal Zone, just a short drive from the downtown area.

On the way in, he explained, "We are going into the depths of Panama's subculture. I know most of the people where we are going because I spend a lot of time there. But you have to be careful. Not only is there a fair share of crazy and weird people, but just the fact that we are Americans causes a big problem with some Panamanians."

"Why is that?" I asked. "I thought that the U.S. and Panama had an excellent working relationship."

"For the most part, we do," Joe said, "but you have to realize that we are foreigners in their country. I don't think there is anywhere else on earth that has a situation quite like what exists in this country, although I suppose West Berlin has some similarities."

"What do you mean?" I asked.

He responded, "The Canal Zone is a strip of land ten miles wide stretching from the Atlantic to the Pacific. It virtually cuts the country in half. The Panamanians have absolutely no say in what happens within the zone because it is controlled and governed by the United States. They even have to have a pass to get into the zone.

"How would you feel if the Panamanians, or anyone else for that matter, controlled a ten-mile-wide strip of land from Canada to Mexico right through the heartland of America? And you couldn't get from one side of the U.S. to the other without a pass! That situation exists here, and these people have to live with it for another thirty-seven years, until the turn of the century. Personally, I cannot blame them for being resentful.

"At any rate," Joe continued, "as long as you realize that this is their country and you show respect, you probably will not have a problem. What generally happens is that the service personnel or new civilians to the Canal Zone tend to forget that. The zone is as American as Kansas, and they walk out as if they have stepped from one state into another. But they have stepped into another country and an entirely different world. You should be able to understand that because you have been living in that circumstance for the last few months."

"You have a way of driving home a point," I said.

"Well, Connie and I have lived in Panama for fifteen years now, and except for occasional trips back to the states, we call this home. I've come to love this country, but I hurt inside because I can see what we, the Americans, are doing to it. Our influence and interference in Panama will one of these days blow up in our faces.

"I, and those of us who have been here for many years, can see the transformation taking place. But we can't do anything about it. We are here until the year 2000, and in the meantime the Panamanians will grow more resentful and militant. I guess the best we can do is to try to keep the peace and enjoy this country while we are here which, incidentally, is just what I plan for you."

"What are you talking about?" Dave countered. "Where are you taking us?"

"To the local whorehouse," Joe said.

Actually, Joe took us to more than one whorehouse. He was a local legend around the circuit. Apparently, he liked to spend a lot of time with the ladies and seemed to know them all personally. He explained, "Panama is a tremendous melting pot of nationalities. Because of the canal, ships from all over the world are continually coming and going, and crewmen from every nation are passing through. These men have been on the high seas for weeks, and by the time they hit port, they are ready for a good time. Most of the time this includes wine, women, and sometimes song.

"In order to satisfy this continual stream of horny men, Panama has an amazing array of women. You can find just about any nationality of woman here," he said. "And if you cannot find what you are looking for, come back in a few weeks. The girls here usually stay for about six months; then they are rotated to another part of the world. It's like a huge syndicate. And there are different classes of whorehouses. There are the cheap five-dollar girls for the majority of the crew, and the fifteen-dollar girls for the staff. Whether you want a Chinese, Italian, Peruvian, American, German, or whatever — you'll find it here."

The day was turning to dusk when we entered the first house. Joe parked the Fiat in a space behind the house and entered through a back door. He opened the door rather abruptly and caught one of the girls by surprise. She was standing in front of a stove stirring some soup as we entered the kitchen. She was wearing only her bra and panties, but the minute she recognized Joe, she dropped her spoon and ran to him, flinging her arms around his neck. She was babbling in some foreign language that I don't think even Joe understood, but at the moment, I don't think he cared either. He introduced us to "Rochelle" and never did bother to tell us where she was from.

We walked from the kitchen into the parlor, but as the hour was still early, no one was there. "No problem," Joe said, and led us upstairs. He barged into one room after another, catching the girls in all sorts of situations, from taking a nap to taking a shower. In every instance, and regardless of whether or not they were wearing clothes, they embraced him.

Joe seemed to be more of a friend than a patron. The girls all greeted him and treated him with the utmost courtesy. He would introduce Dave and me, and they would bow slightly or take our hand, and it was obvious that any friend of Joe's was a friend of theirs. There was no impropriety, just a matter of Joe going around town and saying hello to old friends.

Joe knew them all. He took us to the two finest houses in town and then worked his way down the ladder. As he got into the lower-class houses, he spent less time; he obviously preferred the upper-crust ladies. However, he still knew them all by name.

Joe had made a point of explaining that this night was strictly for introduction and visiting. If we wanted any action, we would have to come back on our own time, a point he reiterated several times. We told him that he didn't have to repeat himself because we were not interested in the activity anyway. At that, he looked at us quizzically and winked, as if to say, "Sure, you bet, I understand."

Actually, seeing some of the girls in the better houses led me to question my sanity. They were beautiful, they were sexy, and they were cheap. But not cheap enough. Money always seemed to be a problem with us.

Later in the evening, we stepped into one of the upper-class houses. From the front door, a short hallway opened to a large parlor that had been converted to a bar. The bar was positioned between two hallways, which led back to a huge room. Only a cocktail waitress and a bartender were at the bar. Looking down the hallway toward the room, I could see dim lights and hear lots of noise, like a huge party was going on. As we entered, the bartender said, "Good evening, Mr. Young. How are you this evening?"

Joe replied, "Fine, Carlos, thank you. How's the action?"

Carlos said, "Not bad for a Wednesday night. Russian Navy is passing through. Those guys are crazy."

Joe turned to us and said, "Let's go see."

We walked down the hallway to the right of the bar and stepped into the large room. It was absolute chaos. There were sailors everywhere, of all different nationalities, all in uniform. The music was loud, and the girls were wild. Most of them were scantily clad, and a few of them were dancing with someone totally naked. Nobody seemed to mind — it was like a giant orgy.

The three of us walked around for a short time and then became separated. I stepped back into a corner to watch. After a few minutes, one of the girls approached me. She appeared to be around twenty years old, heavily made-up, and of Latin origin. She was wearing a man's oversized V-neck tee shirt, and nothing else. Her body was voluptuous, with large breasts swaying beneath the tee shirt and long, slender legs. She moved against me and put her elbows against the wall directly above my shoulders, pressing her body against mine. There was no way I could avoid her, nor did I want to. She began to speak in Spanish, and although I could not completely follow her rapid-fire speech, I understood enough to know that she was asking me to accompany her upstairs.

She was a beautiful woman, but her heavy make-up took away from her glamour. I couldn't help but notice, because she was getting as close to me as possible. Her body had me pinned against the wall, and her face was nose to nose with mine. My hands had been dangling at my sides, and I brought them up onto her back in response to her hands moving around my neck. Out of curiosity, I let my hands move down her back. As I reached the hem of her tee shirt, I realized she had no panties on. At that moment, she stuffed her hand inside my pants. She caught me totally by surprise, for I was not expecting such a fast reaction. She continued her shotgun monologue, very little of which I could comprehend, and started to massage me.

At that moment, I felt a hand slap my right shoulder and, glancing around, saw Joe standing beside me with a grin on his face. "What I said was that if you want to mess around, you can do it on your own time. Let's blow this joint. Tell her you'll come back another night, if that is what you want. I have several more places to take you to." I was not sure whether I was happy or sad that he got me out of that predicament, but I realized that he probably saved me from a case of venereal disease.

I could not understand why Joe was so adamant about not allowing Dave and me to indulge. I thought it was because he considered this to be a sightseeing trip, and that we were on his time. If we wanted to get involved, we would have to do so on our own time. The more I thought about it, the more reasonable it seemed. On the other hand, though he never admitted it, Joe was obviously a good customer to many of the girls. Although he pointed the way, he never let us get close to his activities at any of these establishments. We assumed it was a part of his private life that we were not invited to get to know.

We moved around town from house to house. The differences between the classes of customers and houses were amazing. The cheap whorehouses were small and dirty, with lots of beer being splashed around. The houses smelled bad, and the clients were dishevelled and dirty and smelled bad themselves. The girls were either skinny or overweight and obviously had seen better days.

The middle-class houses were a bit more dignified, with a clientele that was not quite as rowdy. The patrons tended to drink hard liquor, and the girls were better-looking with nicer figures.

The top-of-the-line whorehouses, like the one we had just left, were obviously a cut above. Whereas the girls in the cheapest houses were mostly black, and probably local, the two top "Grade A" houses had a smattering of all skin colors. Black, white, yellow, or anything in between could be found there. And these girls were beautiful. I could not understand how so many gorgeous women from all parts of the world could end up in a place like this.

On the way back to Joe's house later that night, he detoured from the direct route to show us something that he felt was a Panama original. He called it "the world's first drive-in whorehouse."

On the way to the facility, Joe explained that at times the need arose for certain people to be discreet in their activities. This whore-house was designed with that in mind. It was like an eight-unit motel complex, with a garage for each unit. Each garage had both a front and back door with driveways leading to streets front and rear. Clients made appointments by phone and could reserve any unit for any number of hours. A strict timetable was adhered to. Joe told us that the girls in these units were absolutely the finest in the world and were checked regularly for diseases. They were also rotated every three months in order to accommodate this class of clientele with plenty of variety.

Upon approaching the unit at the scheduled time, the garage door would open. The client would drive up the driveway and into the garage. An automatic garage door opener would immediately close the door behind the car. The client would then get out of his car and approach the door to the room. At the bottom of the door was a slot large enough for a tray of food to be passed through.

Clients could, in advance, order food, wine, or champagne, and an attendant would deliver it. The attendant did not know who was inside, since he could not see through the slot. He could see the car and license plates, but anyone seeking anonymity could use a rental or a borrowed car. Joe told us that nonpayment for a visit was never a problem, because the girls controlled the garage door to let the car out. He also explained to us that this house of ill repute was the only one we would not go inside.

We returned the next day to Colón in another attempt to secure passage to Colombia. We found one ship, the *Laguna*, that was willing to take us to the Isla del Rey for a reasonable price. But we would only be part way to Colombia and at the mercy of the next ship's captain. Since we were not having much luck finding other transportation, we seriously considered that option.

During the process of attempting to arrange passage through the canal, Dave and I got to talking about our return trip once we finally arrived at Pucón, Chile. It occurred to us that in order to ensure our return to the United States, we could purchase airline or ship tickets in Panama. We could get any combination of transportation from Santiago or Valparaíso, Chile, back to the states.

Our original intention was to do this anyway, since we did not want to travel the return trip on the same highway that we had taken so far. Besides, we did not have time to drive the return trip from Chile to the United States. We anticipated crating the bikes in Chile and having them freighted back to Portland, Oregon, when we were ready to return.

So, as we attempted to arrange passage to Colombia, we also began checking on various modes of transportation for the return.

After several days of considering different plans, we decided to book passage on a cruise ship from Valparaíso back to Panama. The cruise ship was used primarily by South Americans and, we were informed, was far from "top of the line." But that suited us fine. The trip from Panama back to the states would be via Air Panama, which would fly us to Miami, Florida. This was the cheapest transportation we could find, and we figured we would worry about getting from Florida to Oregon once we set foot on U.S. soil.

We purchased an open booking on Air Panama, which meant that we paid for a ticket but did not book any particular flight. That way, we could be flexible and, upon our return to Panama, could arrange the particular flight we wanted.

We were now secure with the knowledge that, once we reached our destination, we could at least get back to Florida. Our major problem was going to be money. Once we had finally paid for passage through the canal, we were down to slightly over $500 apiece for the rest of the trip. It was going to be a frugal journey!

We finally managed to book passage on the *Salinas* from Colón to Buenaventura, Colombia. We were a little disappointed in the destination, for it meant that we would bypass most of Colombia. We had originally intended to dock in Venezuela or Cartagena, Colombia, near the Venezuela-Colombia border. This original plan would have allowed us to travel the length of Colombia, but due to time restrictions and the matter of the construction at the canal, we were satisfied with the transportation we had secured.

Two days remained before the ship would load our bikes and allow us to board, so we decided just to enjoy Panama City, content with the knowledge that in a few days' time we would be in South America and resuming our trip south.

The few days in Panama City were an opportunity for us to clean our equipment and prepare the bikes for a long, hard push through South America.

We had heard, and were therefore expecting, that roads in South America made the highway through Central America look like a freeway. Preparing for the worst, we purchased new tires for the bikes and gave them full tune-ups.

Furthermore, we knew that the terrain would be much more varied. From sea level to jungles to high in the Andes, we had to be prepared for all kinds of weather and driving conditions.

Those last two days were also spent stocking up on supplies for the rest of the journey. One item we had trouble finding was bug repellent, which we had come to depend on heavily. Joe offered to pick us up several cans at the Canal Zone PX, solving that supply problem. In parts of the countryside, the mosquitoes were fierce. We could not figure out how the native population could survive without some sort of protection. In other areas, the flies were so thick and so much a part of life that apparently they became unnoticed. Like the pictures in *National Geographic* of African children with flies crawling all over them, the same could be seen here. Dave and I could not stand it and found bug spray to be our only relief.

Since Dave and I had been staying in the poorer sections of the towns we visited, we began to make some general observations about the people with whom we were sharing space.

These people were depressed, truly depressed, both economically and socially. There was a dual-class system among all the Latin American countries through which we had passed, and the class distinction was very defined. I suppose, in a way, it could be compared with life in the lower echelons of American society, but there were some differences. In these countries, the oppressed and suppressed classes were definitely the majority. The upper class — the people with money — were a small part of the population. There was no middle class. A citizen either had status or did not. Even the neighborhoods expressed the difference.

The downtown sections and nicer neighborhoods had wide boulevards with lots of trees and expansive sidewalks. Streets were paved or concrete and usually in good shape. The rest of the cities, which contained most of the populace, had roads constructed of brick or just plain dirt. The roads were rough, and chuckholes went unnoticed. The sidewalks were narrow, if there were any, and telephone poles took up much of the sidewalk space. Most of the buildings were constructed of a combination of wood and plaster, with only a few stone and metal structures.

Through all of this, however, the local citizenry maintained a cheerful attitude. They were happy with life because they were here to live it, and they made the most of it. Regardless of the country we were in, we developed a fondness for these people.

We had been in Panama City for two full weeks, and it was time to move on. The freighter was scheduled to leave the pier at midnight the following evening. That day, we were busy purchasing the last of our supplies and getting everything packed into the saddle boxes. We dropped by Joe Young's house just as he was returning home from work and said our goodbyes. He knew that we would be shifting from sea to air travel in Panama City on our return from Chile, and we promised to look him up at that time.

Although we had made the drive from Balboa to Colón several times in the last week, this time it felt different. We knew it was our last trip, and we were anxious to get on with our travels.

Upon arriving at the pier late in the afternoon, we checked with the shipping agent to make sure all was in order. The agent told us to find the foreman and confirm that the bikes were securely tied down once on board. We found him and watched as a crane hoisted the motorcycles and lowered them into the hold.

Once on board, we were pleasantly surprised. The *Salinas* was

My motorcycle being hoisted onto the ship for passage through the Panama Canal and on to Colombia.

a moderate-sized freighter under British flag with an English-speaking crew. Two other couples had boarded in Caracas and were traveling on the ship as far as Valparaíso. Since the ship could only carry seven passengers, we completed the roster.

The ship left at midnight, and we were disappointed about passing through the locks at night. We had hoped to watch the passage. As it turned out, our concern was unfounded. Because of heavy traffic through the canal and congestion caused by the maintenance work on the other side, we anchored prior to entering the first set of locks. We were scheduled to begin the passage early the next morning.

Although we spent only three days aboard the ship, it was a pleasant change from our normal daily routine. The crew was exceptionally accommodating and treated the passengers with every courtesy and convenience. Dave and I finally had to pull our slacks and sportcoats out of the luggage and have them pressed. Meals were white-tablecloth affairs, and dinner two of the three nights was with the captain.

For a couple of guys who each had lost about twenty pounds over the last several months due to a limited diet, this ship was a marvel. Tea was brought to the stateroom at 7:30, breakfast at 8:30, a snack at 11:00, lunch at 1:30, a snack at 4:00, and dinner at 7:00. We tried to take in as many calories as possible, for we knew the ensuing months would be lean.

The ship hoisted anchor before sunrise and began its passage from the Atlantic to the Pacific. This particular crossing would take twenty hours, again because of the heavy traffic and the congestion on the Pacific side.

The day was most interesting for the passengers, and we shot several rolls of film. The ship cleared the Gatún Locks and moved into Gatún Lake. After a short wait while ships passed us traveling the opposite direction, we started again heading southeast. The first few miles found us winding around the lake's islands, a few of which were sparsely settled. The canal then narrowed to the actual channel, beginning in Gamboa. A dredging operation was taking place in the middle of the channel and was probably responsible for some of the shipping delays.

Beyond Gamboa, the ship began its passage of the Gaillard Cut. This section cuts through the mountain range that separates Colón from Panama. The ships travel at eighty-five feet above sea level through a narrow channel, so narrow that it appears that

Ships passing through the Gaillard Cut.

ships approaching from the opposite direction will not be able to pass. Actually, some sections of the channel are only three hundred feet wide, and two-way passage is not possible. The sides of the Gaillard Cut are steep. During construction of the canal, this was the section that was the most difficult and time-consuming to dig. Because of constant slides, re-excavation had to be planned, which added about twenty-five percent to the estimated amount of earth moved.

Clearing the Gaillard Cut, we moved in line to begin our descent back to sea level through the Pedro Miguel locks. It was still daylight as we entered the locks. Lines were thrown from the bow of the ship and tied to the locomotive that pulled us into position into the Miraflores locks. Lowering through these locks took us down to sea level, and a short distance through the dredged channel set us on a course toward Colombia.

Exiting the locks, the ship crossed under the Thatcher Ferry Bridge, which was one of the last segments of construction associated with the canal. Completed in 1962, just one year before our journey, it provided an important and vital link in the Pan-American Highway.

Looking back over the stern of the ship, the bridge sparkled with lights provided for the safety of the ships at night. Looking over the bow, the lights of the clusters of ships awaiting their turn at passage through the canal shone bright against the darkness of the night sea.

The next evening at dinner, the captain pointed out to us that, because of the configuration of the canal's geography, our passage from the Atlantic to the Pacific was actually a trip from west to east. The isthmus has a slight "S" curve, and the canal was built in the middle of this "S", reversing the popular perception of the direction of crossing.

Our few days on the ship were a pleasure. We relaxed and were catered to, but an odd sensation overcame us. We looked forward to getting back on the road, even knowing that within a few days of bouncing along the dirt roads through the jungle we would look back at this short cruise and wonder why we had been so eager for it to end. Yet there was that yearning inside, pulling us toward the unknown adventure yet to come.

We were on the eve of embarking on the part of this journey that we had awaited for more than two years — the journey through South America.

chapter nine
Colombia

The ship pulled into the harbor at the Port of Buenaventura early in the evening, but after dark. Before docking, the Colombian customs officials came to inspect the ship and our papers as well, a typical situation that we had come to expect.

The officials boarded the ship, bringing with them two relatives and two friends of the senior inspector. They first demanded drinks for the entire entourage, then confiscated cigarettes and chocolate, and even a few bottles of perfume for the women they had brought on board.

Of course, the proper docking papers, including our passports and visas, were not properly stamped until the bounty had been secured in their pilot boat. Once accomplished, however, and after two hours of drinking and touring the ship, all was found to be in order and the proper documents changed hands.

This episode introduced us to South America, where we found the customs procedures to be much more corrupt than in Central America.

. . .

The motorcycles were lifted out of the ship's hold by a sling suspended from an overhead crane. Immediately upon touching down on the dock, a huge crowd of people surrounded them.

It was as if they had never seen such an animal before, and perhaps they had not. Motor scooters and small motorcycles were common in the larger cities, but large bikes such as ours were unusual.

Our progress through Central America had tended to attract lots of people, mostly kids, who would mob the bikes to get a closer look. From this demonstration, it looked like the same would hold true in South America.

Often when we left the bikes parked in town, we would return to find youngsters sitting on them and leaning over the handlebars in racing position. Many of these kids were gutsy; often, we had to physically lift them off the machines before we could continue.

When we docked in Buenaventura, rain was falling, a very common occurrence in that part of Colombia. We had heard from some crew members about how filthy and depressing Buenaventura was. Compared with some of the areas we had encountered in Central America, however, we found the city to be fairly livable.

The inevitable fight through customs took several hours, but we managed to clear without losing any money or valuables. In fact, we found that clearing customs in major cities was easier than in remote areas. In the more populated areas, the officials were less prone to delays for they had many people to process. Furthermore, there were always people in line behind us watching the proceedings, thereby minimizing the risk of extortion.

Our problem for the delay at this customs station revolved around the customs carnets. The officials did not want to allow the motorcycles into the country, and when we produced the carnets, they had to check with superiors in Bogotá to find out what those documents meant.

We finally cleared customs and officially began our ride through South America. From Buenaventura, we headed southeast toward Cali under a hard rain. The road was compacted dirt, but was tough going because the continual rains had eroded the edges of the road and created rivulets, which often turned into ditches, across the road.

Even four-wheeled vehicles would have had trouble on this road. The countryside was dense jungle, and as we started rising into the coastal mountains, the roadside waterfalls became frequent, about three to the mile.

At one point, when the rain was falling particularly hard, a waterfall was spilling directly onto the roadway and had to be driven through. Where the waterfall hit the road the surface was a mess, and we figured that crossing an hour later under those conditions would be impossible.

The ride was wet, but we thoroughly enjoyed it anyway. It felt good to be back in the saddle again, and we eagerly anticipated the scenery and experiences that lay ahead.

By the time we reached Cali, ninety miles from our port of entry, the rain had stopped. The sun briefly broke through a thick overcast and shone onto a city nestled on a wide plain. It was a beautiful sight and a beautiful city, clean and modern but with little apparent activity and almost no traffic.

We expected heavy rains that night, and therefore decided to check into a cheap room for the evening. And cheap it was. After our first full day in South America, we determined that if the cost of goods and services we had experienced so far did not change, we would be okay money-wise. The room that night cost twenty cents apiece. In the United States, a wino would have had second thoughts about staying there, but it did provide a mattress and a toilet at the end of the hall, and it was dry — more or less. Besides, we had become accustomed to staying in sleazy joints like that.

Gasoline cost thirteen cents a gallon, and even though it was of a low-octane rating, it performed admirably in the BMWs with a few carburetor adjustments. We did find, however, that the fuel lines and fuel filters required regular cleaning.

The meal that evening cost twenty-five cents. We seldom ate in restaurants, but when we did, it was usually in the larger cities. On these occasions, we would seek the smallest, most inconspicuous places we could find. We didn't get epicurean delights, but we did receive satisfying meals that were a pleasant departure from our normal open-fire cooking. A typical meal might consist of tacos, pollo (chicken), or bistec (beefsteak) with papas fritas (fried potatoes) and a soft drink. Coca-Cola and Pepsi were everywhere throughout Latin America, and consumption was high.

Before this trip — even through the planning stage — I had not given much thought to Colombia. The drug era was in its infancy in 1963. Although Colombia was already known as a source of cocaine, several years would pass before the country would gain its worldwide reputation for sin and vice related to the drug. I thought what most people did: that if hundreds of people were brutally murdered there every year, then it must be a rough and dirty country. We heard stories while we were in the country of four Americans, three nuns and a priest, being hacked to death by machetes near Bogotá. Although we did not confirm the story, we accepted it because Colombia had that sort of reputation. Its social and political reputation spilled over into a general image of the country that was unpleasant.

Contrary to popular perception, however, we found Colombia to be a beautiful country. Dense jungle gradually gave way to gently rolling plains that became the foothills to the Andes mountains, rising 10,000 to 15,000 feet in majestic formations.

And the people were special. Similar to other South Americans, they were shy and reserved, often keeping a distance from us, but upon introduction proved to be helpful and kind. Our appearance was foreign to anything they had ever known, and it was natural that they should be reluctant to approach us. They often stood at a distance and stared at us, probably wondering what we were all about but lacking the nerve to approach.

We were substantially taller than the average citizen and had lost weight on our journey. Our clothes, which were by now well-worn, hung on our frames as if on coat hangers. On top of that, there was Dave's beard. It was really ugly. His few patches of hair had grown to several inches in length and looked absolutely awful.

Fortunately, for those of us who had to look at him, he soon tired of the weird stares and shaved it off. Thereafter, he prided himself in ridiculing me about the beard I was cultivating. I let mine grow on the premise that when you have a face like mine, you should cover as much of it as possible. Dave could not argue with that, so we reached a truce.

Leaving Cali, we headed south through Popayán for the Colombia-Ecuador border. The weather turned dry and beautiful, with sunny skies and mild temperatures. The roads dried out, and we found ourselves driving at high speeds over hard-packed dirt and gravel.

This was the continuation of the Pan-American Highway, and we began to enjoy the ride immensely. The road was fairly smooth with an occasional washboard surface, which could often be avoided by shifting to either side where the water runoff had created a shallow trough. As we started rising into the mountains, the road inevitably became a series of curves and twists, often consisting of several consecutive switchbacks. It had been grooved by prior traffic, and through the turns thousands of tires had pushed the dirt to the outside, creating sizable banking turns.

Powering through these turns, the bike would ride up on the rim like a car on a test track, and the rear wheel would dig in and nearly catapult the machine through the turn. Other vehicles were scarce, with only an occasional truck or bus. Oncoming vehicles could be heard well in advance, which provided a safety factor for our driving style.

We spent several days touring the countryside of southern Colombia. It was so much fun driving these roads and the landscape was so fantastic, a lush green tropical wonderland, that we did not want to leave. We took many short side trips to small towns or points of interest, to prolong our trip through the countryside. As the road dropped out of the mountains to lower elevations, we occasionally passed through sections of dense jungle.

On one of our side trips through this region, we had a frightening experience. Dave was leading the way, and I was following approximately fifty yards behind. All of a sudden, I saw his bike jerk violently. At the same time, his right hand reached up and slapped his neck just below the base of his helmet, right at the collar line. Within about half a minute, his steering became erratic, his bike weaving from one side of the dirt road to the other. His speed began to slow, then his brake light flashed on. He maneuvered to the right shoulder, and with his bike barely in motion, tipped over to the right, falling off his bike into the dense jungle, which started at the very edge of the road.

I was by his side in seconds. His left leg was pinned under the bike, but that wasn't what concerned me. He was lying motionless, and little red dots covered his face, hands, and arms. It looked as if he had suddenly contracted chickenpox. He was breathing somewhat erratically and was not responding to my voice.

Checking to make sure his leg was okay, I removed him from under the motorcycle, dragging him to the edge of the road. We had not seen another vehicle for probably half an hour, nor a house or person for even longer. I didn't know what to do. I couldn't leave him — there was no telling how far away help was. So I did what I could to make him warm and comfortable.

I unrolled his sleeping bag alongside the road and rolled him as gently as possible onto it. Placing his riding jacket under his head, I noticed he was beginning to sweat around his temples.

I took a rag, drenched it with canteen water, and mopped his forehead. With the warm air temperature and those red dots all over his face, it was hard to tell if his body temperature was rising. As I checked him over, I did not notice anything odd, such as a bite on his neck. But when I checked under his shirt, down his back, I found a bee, or something that resembled a bee. It was small and had a reddish color to its body and legs. Apparently, Dave nailed it when he slapped his neck, because the bee was dead.

I waited, pacing and mumbling and wondering what to do next. About an hour later, I noticed that the red dots seemed to be fading. Soon, they began to disappear. Once they were completely gone, Dave regained consciousness and asked what had happened. He didn't remember a thing, other than the bite itself, so we shrugged it off as a weird experience, climbed back on the bikes, and started moving.

That was the only such incident we had during the entire trip.

Beyond Popayán, the road began its ascent into the high country, south through La Unión and Pasto. Southern Colombia took on a beautiful, pristine landscape, very lush and green.

The dirt-and-gravel highway wound its way through the high hills that soon turned into the Western Cordillera of the Andes mountains. Several miles of travel were often necessary to gain one mile of straight-line distance. The road not only wound around, switching back and forth through the foothills, but soon began a serious assault on the mountain range.

From 4,000 feet to 11,000 feet, back to 6,000 feet, returning to 10,000 feet, twisting and turning like this all day long, we ran atop ridges and alongside cliffs, dropping and rising. Looking at the landscape from a distance, it seemed nearly impossible that a road could have been constructed. Although the road was definitely fun to drive, there was one troublesome aspect — no guardrails between the road and drop-offs that sometimes sheered down five hundred to six hundred feet into raging rivers. On several occasions, this condition provided some scary moments.

Everyone along this route, including some Peace Corps volunteers with whom we spoke, commented on the atrocious condition of the roads. We did not say it, but we were thinking, "If they could only see some of the roads that have passed under our tires. We should hope for bad roads like this for the next 10,000 miles." In the back of our minds, we knew this road was a treat, especially considering where we were headed.

chapter ten

Ecuador

A mist lingered most of the morning, except when it was just plain raining hard. We were at high altitudes most of the time and were cold. Both of us wore glasses, which were steamed up all the time. In addition, we had developed head colds. Attending to a runny nose is difficult while wearing gloves and fighting a bad road. In addition, Dave was having trouble with his shock absorbers and generator. As a result, when we entered Ecuador we were expecting the worst. From the standpoint of the roads, we got it.

We cleared customs easily for a change. The Ecuadorans in Tulcán were efficient and professional. It was the first passage through customs that made any sense. The highway was just the opposite — it was awful. Not since Costa Rica had the road been this bad. A portion was bumpy dirt, full of washboard surface, interspersed with cobblestones, many of which were missing. Our top speed on this road was twenty-five miles per hour. Even at that speed, the going was tough.

Between Tulcán and Ibarra, we passed through four villages

that were composed entirely of people descended from African settlers. They seemed very much out of place. We had seen few black inhabitants since entering Mexico, and here were settlements high in the mountains of Ecuador with a truly African flavor. The settlements' houses had thatched roofs and were unlike anything we had seen. The inhabitants were extremely tall and lanky, many of them appearing to be close to seven feet in height.

For this reason, the houses were built with tall doorways and high ceilings — a much different scale than the abodes of these people's much shorter countrymen. In addition, these houses were round and featured exteriors of stick or cane, rather than the mud, stone, or metal-and-cardboard common in the rest of the territory.

As we rode through the hamlets, the kids would rush into the street and block our progress. The first time this happened, we were a bit apprehensive, but upon striking up a conversation with the people we found them to be most hospitable. We told them they must have one hell of a basketball team, but they did not understand. These people, like many in the villages through which we had passed, had no utilities, including electricity. They were technologically isolated from the world and not aware of the cultures and sports of other countries.

For the entire trip, I had looked forward to crossing the equator, but I didn't realize when it finally happened. The day started out with beautiful weather. We could see the high peaks of the Andes rising to over 19,000 feet and the first glimpse of snow-covered peaks since leaving the states.

Shortly after midmorning, the day began to deteriorate. Dave's bike was not running well, I had developed some sort of medical problem that left big red splotches all over my body, and the weather turned bad. It was not that we were preoccupied, but somewhere around Cayambe we passed the monument marking the equator. We drove right by, hardly noticing it. Looking back later that morning, we remembered a monument situated in the middle of the road, splitting it into two lanes, one on either side of the structure. This had not struck us as unusual, for we had seen many such arrangements already, and we had not paid particular attention to this one as it was tarnished and surrounded by weeds. But upon reflection, we realized that we had passed right by one of the highlights of our trip without even stopping to take a picture.

At any rate, we were now in the southern hemisphere. We had started this trip at latitude 45 degrees north and would be ending at latitude 40 degrees south, so in one sense we were approximately halfway. We knew, however, that the roads from here on would be terrible and that we would be making a lot of side excursions. Therefore, in terms of a distance and time, we were still well under halfway. We were now into our fourth month on the road.

We arrived in Quito in a downpour. Being close to the equator, it is usually mild in Quito, but this day was cold, which is understandable for a city sitting at an elevation of nearly 9,500 feet. Dave's bike needed repairs, and we anticipated being in the city for several days, so after locating the BMW shop and a hotel, we acquainted ourselves with the town.

Quito, the oldest of South America's capitals, was the center and capital city of several Indian groups including the Quito. The

Whole towns were constructed with no central water or sewage system, and often with no electrical utility. This town in South America smelled of raw sewage.

Incas annexed the city during the sixteenth century, and seventy-five years later the Spanish conquered the area. Guayaquil developed into Ecuador's chief economic city during the twentieth century, leaving Quito as a historic and serene metropolis. Laid out in a rectangular grid, the city originally was developed by the Indian nations. The architecture reflected the Spanish baroque influence, but Indian and modern styles were also prevalent. Different styles often intermixed within a single building or wall.

But Ecuador is a poor country, and Quito had more than its share of homeless people and bums. Everywhere we went, street people pestered us for handouts, while kids mobbed us. They followed us everywhere, surrounding us every time we stopped. And we were continually stared at. At first, I thought Dave's beard must have been the reason, but then I remembered that he had shaved.

Even the children had to carry their own weight.

Surely it wasn't mine?

We drove to the top of Cerro Panicero, which rises six hundred feet above the city, to get a panoramic view. We found here, as throughout South America, that the slums dominated the higher areas. In the United States, by contrast, this would be the more desirable residential area.

Dave's motorcycle took three days to fix, which allowed us some quiet and peaceful moments. We knew we would need the rest for we had a lot of hard riding to do.

The BMW motorcycle mechanics we encountered were fairly competent. We found these shops only in the largest cities of each country, sometimes associated with a car dealership. The problem was parts availability. The dealerships normally had an inventory of the parts necessary for a tune-up or common maintenance items, such as clutch cables. But if the problem required internal engine parts, it could be weeks before the parts could be delivered. Fortunately, all our repair problems were fairly standard.

Once back on the road, the first section had us passing back over the Andes, reaching an elevation of 15,000 feet, and then dropping down to the coastal city of Guayaquil. Naturally it rained, and the road was a sloppy, gooey mess.

Descending the Andes, even in the rain and mist, was breathtaking. At one point, we were traveling between two layers of clouds, one at 5,000 feet and another at 20,000 feet. Pockets of light, humid mist were interspersed along the road, and we periodically passed through these small ground-level clouds. Emerging from the mist, we beheld panoramas of dense jungle, with banana and papaya trees occasionally along the roadside.

We did not have much luck when we reached Guayaquil. The city was filthy, with bums everywhere and garbage strewn all over. The homeless were using the streets for bathrooms and with 500,000 people and virtually no sewage system, the smell was incredibly bad. It was hard to believe that people could live like this. The populace was continuously beset by disease due to the squalor and filth. Men would urinate against the sides of the buildings with no regard for privacy. Women could often be seen squatting next to a curb or a building with a trickle of fluid running from underneath their dresses. It was deplorable, but these people stayed because it was easier to find food in the city.

Our easiest route to the Peruvian border was by ferry. We arrived in Guayaquil Saturday evening and decided against taking the Sunday ferry, thus avoiding paying overtime for the loading of the bikes. But after two nights in Guayaquil, I felt we would have been better off leaving town earlier. Besides, they hooked us good for loading the bikes anyway. We could have driven up the ramp, but "regulations" required four dockhands (all individually hired) to load. And then the dockmaster nailed us for an additional charge.

The ferry ride itself was a one-of-a-kind experience. Like the pictures you see of boats in the Far East, the craft was a dilapidated old tub absolutely cram-packed with people. The trip was long — more than six hours — and we spent the entire time sitting on a hard wooden bench.

chapter eleven

Peru

Once again, customs was a nightmare. We disembarked the ferry at 4 a.m. and had to wait until 8 a.m. for the Ecuadoran government to check us through to the border. From the dock to the Peruvian border was a drive of less than fifty miles, but the road was awful, in places having eight inches of dust for a roadway.

We arrived at the border a few minutes past noon and knew that we would have a long wait for the border guards to return from lunch. At 2:30 p.m., we began the customs process. It took an hour. Within the next twenty miles, we passed through fifteen police and customs checkpoints. At every one of these stations, we were required to show our documents.

The officials were so slow. Many of them were only slightly literate. They got along fine with common documents with which they were familiar, but our foreign papers confused them. As often as not, they would stamp the papers, usually in the wrong place, as a show of complete understanding. At times, the scene was almost comic.

Another thing we could not figure out was why the main customs stations had strict hours of 8 a.m. to 5 p.m., with a two-hour midday closure, while the roadside checkpoints seemed to be open all hours of the day and night.

We were still hampered by guards occasionally trying to extort money or a watch, but found that making a big show of writing down the guards' badge numbers and taking copious notes of the incident eventually changed their minds.

The Pan-American Highway through Peru proved to be a good road. Stretched out along the coast, it was paved much of the way. The scenery changed from desert to jungle to seashore, but without exception the road was straight and fast. The only unpleasant part of the ride over the first week in Peru was the bugs — they were everywhere, and big.

We spent an enjoyable week, sleeping under the stars among the sand dunes along the coast. As the road moved inland, the altitude rose and we passed through long stretches of desert.

In the afternoon, when the wind would kick up, flying sand was a problem. We couldn't decide which was worse — the sand or the bugs.

This section of Peru, particularly along the coast, had a number of shantytowns, which were large communities, sometimes with thousands of inhabitants. They were cities only in the sense that they contained large numbers of people. Otherwise, there were no services.

The houses were made of cardboard, sticks, pieces of plywood or tin, thrown together in an effort simply to provide shelter. There

One of the many shantytowns scattered along the Pan-American Highway in northern Peru.

were no sewer systems, no central water systems, and in many cases no electricity. Other than a few run-down fishing boats, there appeared to be no visible means of support for the inhabitants.

Many of these impromptu cities seemed to extend forever. They lacked any semblance of city planning, and the roads twisted and turned between the rows of shacks. Road signs were completely absent, and finding a way through these towns was via the guess-and-be-damned route.

Throughout Central and South America, we noticed that different regions, and even certain cities, had peculiar smells that were unique to an area. Riding a motorcycle and being exposed to the elements made this phenomenon more obvious. These cities along the coast of Peru, with the lack of sewage systems and the dry climate, had a stench that was nearly unbearable. But I suppose when you live with it all your life, you become inured. The residents hardly noticed, but it choked us up.

It took us nearly a week to get from the border to Lima. The distance was not terribly far, and the road was good, but we messed around a lot. We spent pleasant mornings swimming and evenings sleeping among the sand dunes along the coast. In contrast, our evenings in the desert were spent securing the tent to withstand the high winds that would pick up just after dark. By midnight, the sand would whip around the tent, trying to work its way in through the seams and any available openings.

About fifty miles from Lima, we came upon the wreckage of a bus and a truck that had collided head-on during the night. Fortunately, the bodies had been cleaned up but witnesses told us that five of the twenty-one bus passengers had been killed. It was easy to see why. Pieces of metal, bus seats, tires from both vehicles, and broken glass were scattered along both sides of the highway for a hundred yards. We had seen the derelict wreckage of many vehicles over the past four months, but this was the most recent accident scene we had come across.

Judging from the number of wrecks, it seemed that either they were never cleaned up or there were a lot of accidents for the slight amount of travel on the highway. We decided that both assumptions were probably true.

We had been on the road more than four months when we pulled into Lima. We expected to be there for just a few days to service the bikes and take care of incidentals, but a series of events delayed us nearly a week.

First came a hassle with the U.S. Embassy. We had expected to pick up some mail there that had been confirmed through earlier correspondence. Along the trip, we had been writing a series of articles for the *Oregonian* newspaper and were anticipating receiving the printed copy. We knew it had been sent. Also in the packet was a fully-executed insurance paper we needed in order to clear customs into Chile.

No one at the embassy knew anything about correspondence for us. We visited every day to check on its status. Mitchelson, the ambassador's assistant, was beginning to get on our nerves and we knew we were getting on his. The final day ended in a shouting match among the three of us, with Dave and me stomping out of the embassy building empty-handed.

We had seen some crazy driving on this trip, particularly in Mexico City. But those people didn't hold a candle to the Lima drivers. In 1963, Lima was a city of two million people, and a fair number of those inhabitants were cab drivers. I don't know where they found all the old American cars, but they all drove vehicles called "colectivos." These were American relics of late '40s vintage with no doors, no hoods, and sometimes no trunks. Passengers would pile into these rigs en masse, sometimes cramming up to five in the space that was once a trunk. The college kids of the '60s who tried to see how many could squeeze into a Volkswagen had nothing on these people.

The colectivos ran routes like buses. They would travel about two miles down one street and then double back on another street, crisscrossing all over the city. If you knew the routes, you could get

One of the better-looking "colectivos" serving the commuters of Lima, Peru.

anywhere in town in a short amount of time. The trouble was that you put your life on the line riding in those rigs. The collectivos raced around their routes, packed with passengers and not paying any attention to the few — very few — stoplights and traffic signs. The faster they got to the next stop, the sooner they got more paying customers.

Like Mexico City, Lima had many traffic circles, and the cabbies took considerable delight in seeing who could race around them the fastest. Our driver always seemed to win.

We felt ill the second day in town, so we checked out of our sleazy hotel room and into another sleazy room, this one with its own bathroom. This was a luxury we had forgone since leaving the states, and the timing was fortunate.

Both Dave and I had experienced bouts of dysentery over the past few months, but all of a sudden it hit us both with a vengeance.

The abdominal pains got so severe that at first we were afraid we were going to die, and then later we were afraid we weren't. Our concern was that it might lead to hepatitis. To make matters worse, the mattresses had bedbugs, and we both developed a good set of bites.

During this period of illness, someone broke the locks on my saddle boxes and took about half of my belongings. Why they did not take more is a mystery. But after this incident, we decided to replace the boxes with inexpensive suitcases that we could remove and take with us. We traded the boxes and some of our little-used equipment for some 35mm film and a couple of meals. After the meals, we decided the cook got the better end of the deal.

Leaving Lima was no big disappointment for us. We had some tough luck and rough times, particularly trying to battle back from illness. Still feeling quite queasy, we were nonetheless eager to get moving again.

Our travel from here was about to take a turn. We were to leave the Pan-American Highway and head east, up over the Cordillera Occidental, the western range of the Andes mountains. Our initial destination was Cuzco, where we would head in a southerly direction towards Bolivia.

We anticipated that the toughest part of the ride lay just ahead. The Central Highway through Peru was a dirt road that bounced around through the Andes. What we did not realize was that for the next month we would be spending most of our time more than 10,000 feet above sea level.

At 1:30 in the afternoon, we set out with the new suitcases

strapped to the sides of the bikes. We had checked with the Automobile Club of Lima about road conditions and were expecting 175 miles of pavement before the dirt road started. We got thirty, just before the road began to climb.

By 3:30, we were at nearly 16,000 feet, and the road had deteriorated to not much better than a cow path. The clouds moved in and out, alternating between rain and drizzle. Worst of all, it was cold. My gloves had been stolen, and I had not yet replaced them, which further accentuated the bitter weather. We were disappointed in our progress, having expected better road conditions. Consequently, we ended the day pitching our tent at 15,000 feet, among the snow-covered peaks.

Many more miserable nights were to follow, but that night was memorable because it was the first night I lay awake shivering until dawn. I crawled into the sack fully-clothed and throughout the night kept throwing clothes on top of the sleeping bag in a futile attempt to stay warm. I kept hoping for daylight, thinking that as long as I was awake I might as well be traveling.

Through the mining towns of La Oroya and Huancayo, the road improved, only to revert to decrepitude as the road stretched out from town.

Past Huancayo, the road turned ugly. The next hundred miles consisted of a one-lane dirt path carved into the side of the mountain. It wound along the mountainside, following the river that seemed desperate to get its icy waters to the ocean. Precipitous drops from the road to the river below were standard for this section. The road was so narrow that the infrequent truck or bus traveling this central highway had a hard time squeezing through some of the cuts. Passing oncoming vehicles along this 100-mile stretch was, through many sections, impossible. For this reason, the road had controlled access, with traffic being allowed one direction three days of the week and the opposite direction the other four days.

We arrived at the control station on the afternoon of the day the traffic was oncoming. The timing was good because we could attend to some repairs the rest of the afternoon and then get an early start the following morning. We had not yet adjusted to the 10,000-foot altitude and were both fighting headaches, so being lazy for a few hours seemed like a good idea.

It was another bitterly cold and sleepless night, so we were up early to be at the check-in station when it opened. At 8 a.m., the officials confirmed that the previous day's traffic — two buses and one truck — had cleared, and they checked us in for our passage. We were the only vehicles present, and the officer informed us that he expected only one bus later in the morning.

From recent rain in this region of the Andes, the road was muddy and the going was slow. On two wheels, we were slipping and sliding all over the road. A few times, we slid dangerously close to the edge of the drop-off.

Once in particular, I hit a muddy patch and fishtailed toward the edge. I wasn't going fast, but I could not stop the bike. It just kept sliding. My heart raced as I anticipated going over the edge. Just as my front wheel reached the precipice, my back wheel hit a rock and kicked the rear of the bike around.

Fortunately, I fell to the inside rather than over the cliff. My pride was long past being bruised by such incidents, so the only harm done was that I ended up in the mud. Actually, I let out a big

Portions of the Pan-American Highway permitted high-speed travel . . .

sigh of relief just to still be alive. Going over that precipice and falling one hundred feet into the icy river would have ended my trip permanently.

It took a full day to travel this 100-mile stretch. Except for a tough ride, it was uneventful. We did not see a single person until we exited the section late in the afternoon. Beyond the exiting checkpoint the road improved — a little. At least, it was wider. Before we reached Ayacucho, we had crossed seven streams, three gigantic mud puddles, and ten very long dusty stretches where the dust lay up to eight inches deep on the roadway. Dave took one nasty spill into the dust. After the dust had settled, we could just see the end of one handlebar sticking up. Other than that, it was impossible to know that a motorcycle was lying in the middle of the road.

. . . but normally our progress was slow due to a variety of problems with the roadway. At its worst, it was nearly impassable.

• • •

The one-way section of road ended in Ayacucho, which is one of the many small mining towns scattered along the Central Highway. The mining must have been nonexistent for the only activity was the inactivity of Indians sitting around apparently waiting for something to happen.

Each town had its own farmers' market which usually encircled the small town square. But more often than not, and always on weekdays, we observed more vendors than customers. The other problem was that the roads were so awful that very little transport was possible. A railway penetrated the high country out of Lima, but we spent several days within sight of the tracks and never did see a train.

As we dismounted our bikes in Ayacucho, I discovered that my jacket had dropped off the luggage rack of the bike. I remembered having taken it off when I helped Dave up from his spill in the dust. I wanted to go back and look for it, but the control station would not let me pass as I would have been traveling the wrong direction for that day. So I figured some lucky Indian now had himself a perfectly good coat. Worse yet, the day before I had purchased a set of gloves which were stuffed in the jacket's pockets.

The road leading out of Ayacucho was a decent gravel and dirt mix, a welcome change after the one-way section we had just completed. We did not want to get excited about its condition, though, for we had seen the road surface radically change in the past. Once again, ten miles out of Ayacucho, our expectations were fulfilled. How anyone could seriously call this a highway, or even a road for that matter, was beyond us.

Leaving Ayacucho, we covered forty-five miles in just under five hours. The nine-mile-per-hour average was worse than our most dismal expectation, but the road was horrendous. In many places, it was merely two tire tracks that bumped along the mountainside. The two tracks had been ravaged by the elements and were pocked with chuckholes of immense size. Often we were better off paralleling the road through the countryside rather than trying to maneuver the bikes down the road itself.

Along with the road, we had to fight the cold and the altitude. Since I had not yet replaced my jacket, I bundled up in everything

I could lay my hands on. Fighting the road was enough exercise to keep our bodies warm. At night in the tent, sometimes above 15,000 feet, the cold really seeped in. We would climb into the sleeping bags fully-clothed — boots, sweaters and all — and still could not get warm.

Furthermore, we had not yet acclimated to these altitudes. We were short of breath and had chronic headaches, although they subsided by the end of each day.

On one occasion, somewhere up in the high country, we emerged from the tent one morning to find an Indian standing in front of the tent, about ten feet away. We had just experienced another sleepless night because of the cold, and here was this Indian standing there at 6 a.m. in a lightweight shirt and no shoes.

I am not sure who scared whom the most. We were not expecting company, and he was not expecting gringos. We offered some salutary remarks and soon discovered that, like many Indians throughout the region, he did not speak Spanish.

Several Indian dialects were prevalent, one of the most common being Quechua, and we presumed that to be his language. We went through the ritual of establishing sign language, and he invited us to his home for something to eat. We were a little cautious, for their diets are quite dissimilar to our own, but we decided to go with him anyway.

We walked on a dirt path for about half a mile, over a ridge that had paralleled the road. Walking around a rock outcropping, we abruptly came upon a dwelling made of rocks cemented together with a mud-like substance. The roof consisted of sticks that also were held together with this mortar. There was no door, just an opening, and no windows. The single room was about ten feet on either side and had a fire pit in the middle of the dirt floor.

The only furnishings evident were a straw mattress against one wall and a few cooking utensils hanging from another wall. The entire structure appeared to be used solely for cooking and sleeping. No one was present other than the three of us, although it looked like the Indian had a mate, for some tattered dresses lay folded in one corner. He did have a few goats, however, which were milling around the outside of the dwelling.

We had been apprehensive about this visit because of what we were afraid he would offer us to eat. We soon learned we had every reason to be apprehensive. He left the room for a few moments, returning shortly with a ball of goat cheese about the size of a baseball. The moment he walked through the door we could smell it. It was awful. A rancid odor matched its putrid gray color.

The Indian offered it to us, extending his arms with the cheeseball cupped in his hands. He was obviously very proud of his gesture for his smile broke wide open, exhibiting a semi-toothless grin. We certainly could not hurt his feelings, so we delicately removed the cheeseball from his hands. We attempted to change the emphasis of our conversation, or sign language dialogue, to another matter. But he would have no part of it; he kept gesturing for us to try a piece of his prized cheese.

We had run out of options. I took a small — very small — chunk out of the side of the ball. The cheese had tiny hairs that were not obvious from the outside but once broken apart seemed to permeate the substance. As I lifted this minuscule portion to my mouth, its odor nearly sent me to my knees. But I did the polite thing and set the bit of cheese on my tongue.

I cannot think of another time in my life when I have eaten anything so distasteful. We had experienced some foods on this trip that I had surprised myself by trying — pig-brain soup, for instance. But this morsel of cheese had absolutely the most disgusting taste imaginable.

I managed to swallow, as did Dave. We glanced at one another with an expression of grief over our impending demise. Our problem now was how to avoid taking another bite. We distracted the Indian by getting him to talk about his sandals, which we had spotted hanging from the wall. The sandals were apparently his prized possession. We had seen some like them before on other inhabitants of the region. The soles were made from old tires, with the tread still evident. The straps were made of strips of inner tube sewn to the tire-tread sole. Since this Indian was shoeless, we presumed these to be his Sunday shoes. The ploy worked. We spent a bit more time with him and departed with handshakes and pleasant gestures. As soon as we were out of sight, however, the cheeseball became a projectile. The taste remained with us for days afterward.

As we neared Abancay, the temperature rose even though we were well above 10,000 feet. The road, however, continued to be terrible. We had to make quick decisions: whether to dive into the chuckhole on the right, balance on the mud ridge next to it, bounce our way over the pile of rocks in the center, or splash our way through the mud puddle on the left. Electing none of the above could have meant driving off the edge of the road and freefalling into the river one hundred feet below. This went on for mile after mile after mile.

At one point, we could see the town of Abancay about seven miles distant as the crow flies. But the road wound through the countryside, shifting back and forth, up and down. At certain high vantage points, we could see the road and its nonsensical meandering through the valleys. It looked like a length of yarn wadded up and then dropped onto a piece of green canvas. These meanderings took us thirty miles and two-and-a-half hours to get to Abancay.

The road had an offsetting bonus — the scenery. As the road twisted through the high country, it offered one panorama after another of towering green mountains offset by huge valleys with raging rivers at their base. The vista from 11,000 feet might offer snowcapped peaks at 20,000 feet falling dramatically to valleys at 4,000 feet. And the coloration was spectacular. Brilliant blue skies and gray and brown rock formations offset the variety of dark greens in the mountains.

Wildlife in this high country was scarce. However, an occasional herd of llamas could be seen majestically roaming the mountainsides. And at the higher elevations, usually above 15,000 feet, alpaca could be spotted.

We looked forward to getting to Cuzco for a number of reasons, not the least of which was that we were anxious to get off the Central Highway for a few days, plus I needed to buy some new clothes. Cuzco is a city steeped in history from the days of the Inca Empire and later from the Spanish occupation. Francisco

Pizarro established his residence there, and the city is important from an archeological standpoint. Cuzco is also the departure point for the ruins of Machu Picchu, which we definitely wanted to see.

Since no road leads to the ruins from Cuzco, we had to ride the autocar rail. Until this point in South America, we had encountered only one other English-speaking traveler. This one-car train, however, was crammed full of Americans and other English-speaking people. A quick survey showed that everyone except us had flown into Cuzco. In retrospect, that should not have surprised us. We knew that the larger cities and points of interest were full of tourists. We seldom encountered them because we were traveling in a much different fashion. Besides, over the past week, we had learned the difficulty of getting to Cuzco other than by air.

We had been living among the natives so long that we tended to forget that there was another facet to life in these countries that we had been missing — the upper-class lifestyle. Quite frankly, the few times we were exposed to those travelers staying in the finer hotels and living the upper-crust life, we yearned to get back among the common citizenry. These other travelers would often deride the common folk for their depravity and squalor, condemning these poor people as if they had deliberately chosen their lifestyle. Every time we heard this ridicule, we wanted to get out among the commoners as soon as possible, for we felt comfortable there.

Machu Picchu is located high in the Andes on a ridge between two peaks with the Urubamba River raging nearly 2,000 feet below. Disembarking the train, the visitors boarded a bus which carried us from the level of the river up a steep road with a number of switchbacks. The bus unloaded the visitors in a small turnaround at the entrance to the city. Most of the other passengers, who had flown in from Lima, were complaining of headaches from the high altitude. Fortunately, Dave and I had finally become acclimated. But once inside the ruins, the ancient city's majesty made everyone forget their ailments.

Little is known of Machu Picchu's history. For centuries, but particularly during the fifteenth century, the Inca Empire expanded throughout the high country of what is now Peru, Bolivia, Ecuador, and portions of Chile. They assaulted neighboring rival tribes and built a civilization with these conquered lands and people that developed into a highly organized empire. The domain extended for 3,000 miles and was populated by more than six million people.

In the mid thirteenth to early fourteenth centuries, trouble developed in this magnificent empire. It is believed that during this period huge fortresses were constructed to protect the empire from invaders. The most spectacular of these fortresses was the mountaintop city of Machu Picchu.

The Incan empire was finally destroyed by two factors. First, successors to the empire's throne proved inept and the civilization was thrown into civil war. Second, at that critical time, the Spaniards arrived.

In the early years of the sixteenth century, rumors of fabulous treasures in Peru were circulating among the Spaniards who were then occupying Panama. Many hoped (and a few tried) to plunder the spoils of this enchanted land to the south.

All expeditions were unsuccessful for one reason or another until 1528, when Francisco Pizarro petitioned Charles I and the

The lost city of Machu Picchu was an Incan stronghold situated high in the Andes mountains.

Imperial Court and was granted the resources to effectively invade this land. By that time, the Incan empire was disintegrating from within due to civil strife.

The next ten years were filled with war, massacre, treachery, and incompetence. Pizarro and his invading forces should have easily overthrown the docile and serene Incas. But useless battles with the Indians and infighting among the conquerors led to a long and bitter conquest.

The Spaniards did, in fact, find their valued treasures. In 1532, Pizarro coaxed the ruler of the Incas, Atahuallpa, to visit him in Cajamarca. Atahuallpa arrived, borne on his golden throne and surrounded by 5,000 of his devoted followers and warriors. A lone Spaniard and Pizarro's emissary, the priest Valverde, appeared before the Inca ruler and proclaimed conquest of the empire and demanded submission to the King of Castile and the Pope. Upon completion of the proclamation, the priest passed a prayer book to the Incan which, after a brief translation, was thrown to the ground.

That was the ultimate sin. Pizarro's two hundred men, who had been hiding and lying in wait, opened fire. The unarmed Indians were slaughtered. Thousands died and the Incan ruler was claimed as a prisoner, while not a single Spaniard died or was even severely wounded during the battle.

Atahuallpa knew of the Spaniards' love of gold and silver and ransomed his freedom by promising to fill a room twelve feet by seventeen feet as high as his arm could reach with pure gold. A second room would likewise be filled with silver. Pizarro promised the ruler his freedom and recorded the agreement in writing. Over two months, couriers brought in load after load of gold and silver artifacts, and the rooms were filled as agreed. The gold was melted down in order to be more easily transported and distributed. In the end, about 13,000 pounds of gold and twice as much silver in priceless Incan treasures were destroyed.

Atahuallpa lived up to his part of the bargain. Pizarro did not. He concocted a legal argument that the Inca ruler was guilty of treason by inciting his followers to revolt. The Indian was hastily tried, convicted, and sentenced to be burned alive. However, he was offered a more honorable death by strangulation on the condition that he accept baptism. He accepted, and immediately thereafter was executed.

A few years later, Pizarro was murdered in his home.*

The lost city of the Incas, Machu Picchu, is not mentioned in the writings of the Spanish conquerors, and although there were contemporary stories of the existence of such strongholds, they were never discovered by the invaders. At least, no one ever lived to document such existence. The city eventually was discovered by an American explorer, Hiram Bingham, in 1911.

The ruined city now stands atop the remote mountain hideaway as a tribute to the civilization that once existed there. The city covers about five square miles and consists mainly of terraces built around a central plaza with numerous stairways and paths linking sections of the city.

Most of the buildings are remnants of single-family dwellings. These homes were built around internal courts that functioned as community areas. Larger structures were apparently used for religious ceremonies.

The Incas did not have a written language and so, although they were quite developed as a civilization, their history has to be rebuilt piece by piece, just as the anthropologists and archeologists are putting this city back together stone by stone.

The entire city is distinguished by superb engineering and crafts-

---

* Hubert Herring, *A History of Latin America from the Beginnings to the Present*, 2nd ed. (New York: Alfred A. Knopf, 1964).

Looking down on Machu Picchu from the summit of Huanya Picchu.

manship of construction. All the dwellings and buildings were built from large rocks which were crafted in a manner that fit them together like a jigsaw puzzle. No mortar was used between the rocks. Even today, the rocks fit together so snugly that the blade of a pocketknife cannot be shoved between them.

A highway (part pavement, part cobblestone) runs through the city's center, originally constructed to connect different areas of the Incas' realm. The city had been self-sustaining and had an estimated population of 1,000 at its peak, even including a water causeway which transported water to the city from the surrounding mountains.

Since the city straddled a ridge high in the mountains, terraces were constructed on the steep slopes for buildings and for the cultivation of food. At one end of the ruins, a peak rises eight

After the ruins were discovered in the early 1900s, some of the structures were rebuilt. Today, the site is a popular attraction in the Peruvian highlands.

hundred feet above the city. The peak is called Huanya Picchu and has the characteristic terraces of the rest of the metropolis.

We climbed the steep pathway leading to Huanya Picchu's summit and found a spectacular view that looks out over the ruins and the Urubamba River valley. At one place at the summit, an unprotected ledge drops vertically to the river several thousand feet below.

While we were at the summit, a search party arrived. Earlier in the day, two Mormon missionary students apparently had climbed to the spot where we stood. They had separated at the top, each exploring a different section of the upper ruins. Shortly thereafter, one student could not find the other. Assuming his partner had descended the pathway to the lower city, he went there to look. When he could not find his friend, the search party was organized.

We spent most of the day at the ruins. The entire time, the search party continued its quest. It crossed our minds that if someone got too close to the edge of that unprotected ledge, he could slip and fall into the raging river below. When we left that day, the lost missionary's whereabouts were still unknown.

Two months later, while we were in Santiago, Chile, we read in a newspaper that a body, identified as that of a Mormon missionary, had washed up on the shore of a river in the Amazon jungle. The Urubamba River flows east into the Amazon jungle.

We returned to Cuzco and spent a few enjoyable days investigating its history and the ruins that are throughout the city and the surrounding region. A week earlier when we left Lima and headed for Cuzco, we were hampered by a strike by the federal employees who deliver gasoline. Refilling our fuel tanks had become an exercise in frustration. We were bleeding the last few drops out of station hoses in the major cities along the highway and begging, borrowing, and buying fuel from anyone who had even a pint.

The strike was still in effect as we prepared to leave Cuzco, and we were fortunate to run across a meteorologist who worked for Panagra, Peru's national airline. He had a barrel of gasoline that he used to power the generators for his equipment, and he was kind enough to share several gallons with us. We were anxious to get rolling; we figured we would worry about additional fuel later. As it turned out, the strike ended the next day.

The road was definitely better leaving Cuzco than it had been arriving. The surface was fairly smooth, but now the dust became bothersome. Dave and I had to revert to traveling five minutes apart in order for the dust from the lead bike to settle. Two problems arose during this stretch of the trip. I developed a cold; with my nose plugged, I had to breath through my mouth. Traveling on a dusty road made this very uncomfortable. Additionally, my lip split from the cold and bled all over my beard. I was not a pretty sight.

The second problem was mechanical. My clutch cable broke and we did not have a spare. I tried to get it fixed in Cuzco, but the best I could do was to have it soldered together. Of course that did not hold, and a few miles out of town it broke. The nearest cable was in La Paz, Bolivia, and we needed to keep moving.

After some discussion, we rigged up an awkward apparatus that worked, though poorly. We tied a length of our nylon rope to the clutch-activating arm that sticks out of the transmission at the bottom of the bike. Then we strung the rope around the crash bar and up and over the handlebars. On that end of the rope we tied a stick, creating a handle similar to that on a water ski rope.

To change gears on a motorcycle, normally the left handlebar is squeezed to disengage the clutch, thereby allowing the driver to shift gears. Now, every time I needed to shift, I had to remove one hand from the handlebars, grab the stick hanging over them, and pull back hard on the rope to complete the shifting function. Under normal driving conditions, it would work satisfactorily. On a South American highway, it was very challenging.

From Lima, along the Central Highway in Peru, we stayed in a few hotel rooms when it was not convenient to pitch the tent. They were always the same — a dingy little room with two small single beds as the only furniture. A bare light bulb suspended from the ceiling by an exposed electrical cord seemed to be in vogue. Some of these hotels even had showers, but only lukewarm water would trickle out of about half the holes in the showerhead. And the showerhead was always directly overhead, so it was tough to get fully wet all at one time.

Furthermore, the Peruvians are not a tall people, on the average. Therefore, we had to duck to get under the showerhead. Nonetheless, those showers always felt great.

Approaching the Bolivian border, we passed along the shore of Lake Titicaca. This is high country and a beautiful setting. Lake Titicaca is the largest lake in South America and the highest navigable lake in the world. It is 110 miles long, thirty-five miles wide, and sits at an altitude of 12,500 feet. Set against the backdrop of the towering, snowcapped Andes peaks, some of which reach nearly 22,000 feet, the region's scenery is spectacular. Lake Titicaca was also one of the seats of early Indian civilization, some of which predated the Incan period, and therefore is rich in architectural and archeological remains.

We arrived at the Peru-Bolivia border and, as expected, had more than our share of trouble gaining passage to Bolivia. This crossing was particularly difficult. One of the officials must not have liked the way we looked or something. At least Dave had shaved off his beard; otherwise, we probably would still be there.

chapter twelve

Bolivia

We looked forward to our ride along the shore of Lake Titicaca. The water was high and had flooded the road in a few places, forcing us, in a way, to drive through the lake.

We had been curious about Bolivia. Many people asked us why we wanted to go there, insinuating that there was little to see. They could not have been more wrong. We found the countryside exquisite, with its high plateaus flanked by towering mountain ranges, and the Indians friendly.

The road was a decent hard-packed dirt surface that allowed reasonable speeds, and was flat and straight for the most part. This region of southern Peru and northwestern Bolivia is the altiplano, a high plateau encompassing a series of intermountain basins between the eastern and western cordilleras (ranges) of the Andes.

Most of the altiplano is at an altitude of 12,000 feet, although portions of it rise to around 14,000 feet. Despite the cold, dry, and windy climate, the area was heavily populated. The Indians of the

Many inhabitants of the Andes high country chew coca leaves, from which cocaine is derived. They wander aimlessly around the mountains in a stupor.

region tried to farm a living off the dry landscape by raising potatoes and barley and by tending herds of llamas.

One of these friendly Indians was a little too friendly. Because of the high water at Lake Titicaca, the streams into and out of the lake were overflowing. One of these streams had flooded the road, and we were looking for a shallow spot to cross to the other side to continue our journey.

An Indian came staggering up to me holding a half-empty

liquor bottle in one hand and one of his rubber sandals in the other. He was having difficulty standing, swaying from side to side, and often backpedaling to maintain his balance. He, like so many of the region's inhabitants, did not speak Spanish but rather one of the Indian dialects, so we had a hard time communicating. I finally got the idea, however, that he was trying to show me a shallow part of the stream to cross. I took his advice and motored across the stream to the other side.

When I turned around to see if Dave was going to make it, I saw the Indian staggering toward me through knee-deep water. The Indian beat Dave across the stream and drunkenly walked up to me. Now I realized what he wanted — money, for having helped me across the stream. If I had had a few coins, I probably would have given him some just to get rid of him. But both Dave and I had only larger bills, and he certainly was not worth that. So I shrugged my shoulders, turning my palms upward in a gesture of "sorry," and prepared to drive off.

This Indian was persistent and was not going to let me get away without paying. He was now facing me head-on, standing directly in front of my motorcycle. As I began to move forward, he reached out and grabbed my handlebars with both hands, tossing aside his bottle and sandals. I continued to inch forward. As I did so, he sat down on my front fender, still clutching the handlebars. I stepped up my forward motion and, with this drunk Indian now sitting on my front fender facing me, tried to coax him off my bike.

He would have no part of it. Dave came over, and together we tried to remove him from the machine. But as we grabbed him, he began yelling and screaming and raising a terrible ruckus. We

Most of the high-country Indians do not speak Spanish, but rather Indian dialects. This fellow climbed onto my fender and I could not get him off.

were out in the middle of the altiplano and no one was nearby so his antics did not attract attention.

Our efforts were useless. Finally, I decided that perhaps I could scare him off the fender. I jumped on the kick starter and began moving forward down the dirt road. He was swaying from side to side but still holding on, and the faster I moved, the harder he held on. Before long I was traveling over the bumpy road at about fifty miles an hour with this drunk Indian sitting on my front fender, bouncing around and holding on for dear life. I was afraid that if he fell off, he might hurt himself or I might run over him.

After several miles, I stopped abruptly. I guess the Indian had had enough. His face was ashen, and he dismounted almost before I came to a complete halt. He looked at me with a little twinkle in his eye and the corner of his mouth curled up just a bit as if to say, "Thanks a lot for the ride, pal." I don't know where he thought he was going, but he left the road and staggered off into the altiplano.

La Paz is a beautiful city, and approaching it as we did was spectacular. The altiplano gradually rises to about 14,000 feet around La Paz. The city itself sits in a valley. As the road drops from the altiplano into the city, a traveler gets a tremendous overview of the entire metropolis. La Paz is the highest major city in the world, sitting at an altitude of 12,000 feet, and the air is thin. People flying in from sea-level cities often suffer several unpleasant days trying to adjust to the altitude.

Perhaps one reason we enjoyed the city so much was that we decided to splurge and get a somewhat nicer room than we were accustomed to — one with a shower and hot water and a few other amenities. We figured we might as well enjoy it, because leaving La Paz was going to mean a long, hard ride to Santiago.

I needed a new clutch cable for my bike to replace the rope we had rigged. The phone book yielded the address of the local BMW shop, but we could not find its location. After driving around for several hours, searching fruitlessly, I asked a man wearing a BMW lapel pin where the shop was, and he directed us there. The

We spent a month above 11,000 feet in Peru and Bolivia. Many of our campsites, like this one, were above 15,000 feet.

automobile dealership was small, with no cars in stock, and the dealer had little knowledge of BMW motorcycles. Nonetheless, he ordered the parts we needed. This meant we had several days to sightsee around the area.

We had heard that the highest ski area in the world was nearby. A few hours' drive from La Paz, Chalcaltaya sits high in the Andes. The dirt road was neglected and badly eroded by melting snow. Once the road got into the snow, however, it became smoother.

Traveling on a snow-packed road on two wheels was difficult, and reaching the ski area was a slow process. The lodge itself, sitting at 17,500 feet, was a beautiful little chalet overlooking the altiplano and valleys. The ski lift was a cable apparatus that pulled skiers to the top of the mountain, above 18,000 feet. The ski area was fairly steep and extended well below the lodge.

In the Bolivian high country, the going got difficult on two wheels. This picture was taken above 17,000 feet.

Since it was the middle of the week, few people were present. We did see one fellow with a pair of Head skis. Upon further inspection, we noticed a Mount Hood, Oregon, ski patch on his jacket. Striking up a conversation, we discovered that he was a college-mate of Dave's at Portland State University and was taking a vacation from his stint in the Peace Corps.

Our last few days in La Paz centered around preparations for the next segment. We had both contracted dysentery again and spent a few days lying around to get over the worst of it. In the meantime, I had taken my bike to the BMW shop to be fitted with the new clutch cable. By the time we were feeling well enough to ride, the part had been received and installed.

We knew we had a tough stretch ahead. The road on our map

led from La Paz to Arica, Chile, which is on the coast at the northern end of the country, just across the border from Peru. The altitude dropped 14,000 feet, and we anticipated rough road conditions. We checked with both the automobile club of Bolivia and the police before setting out. They referred to their maps and confirmed that the road was in good shape. We believed them. After so many months on the road, however, we had developed some skepticism, which turned out once again to be well-founded.

chapter thirteen

The Road to Arica

We gunned across the altiplano, trying to make up for a late start, but after only ten miles had to slow to a crawl because of the deterioration of the road. We had to dodge gullies that crisscrossed the road and rocks that flash floods had left behind. We began to wind our way down off the altiplano and into barren rolling hills, which gradually become the great Western Cordillera of the Andes some sixty miles to the west.

Through one fifteen-mile stretch, the road wound along a river, which we had to cross twenty times without the help of bridges. Dave was the first to get stuck midstream, and we soon got used to water in our boots from pushing the bikes across.

We traveled for six hours straight and covered seventy miles, averaging about thirteen miles per hour. The lingering effects of our dysentery and the hard ride took a toll on us that day. Late in

In places, the Pan-American Highway had no bridges, forcing us to ford rivers.

the afternoon, however, we banged and bounced our way into the little copper-mining town of Corocoro.

Corocoro sits at an elevation of 13,000 feet and is a cold town, with the wind whistling down from the hills of the surrounding countryside. It was hard to keep warm, particularly at night. We had accustomed ourselves to tent-sleeping at these altitudes, but for some reason we were restless that night. Perhaps it was the quietness of the town, with the wind exaggerating the chill in the air, or perhaps it was our uncertainty of what lay ahead.

The following morning we got some gas from the local mining company. The people there were curious about our route from La Paz. They indicated that the bridges had washed out years ago and a much longer but better road had been constructed. They were surprised that we had succeeded in making the passage.

Leaving the mining company, an Indian directed us to the edge of town, pointing out the direction we were to follow in order to reach the town of Charaña. Our destination was Arica, Chile, and Charaña was a small village on the Bolivia-Chile border. It was about one hundred miles away, directly in line with Arica from our present position.

The direction in which the Indian pointed held no sign of any type of road. We were informed, upon further investigation, that no motorized vehicle had made the passage to Charaña in more than ten years. Obviously, this was a time for a decision.

We discussed the possibility of turning back and returning to La Paz. From there, we would re-enter Peru, cross the Andes on a regular road, and pass down onto the coast and into Chile. To do this, however, would require another visa for re-entering Peru and probably an extra week of travel. In addition, the thought of back-tracking on the Central Highway was not a pleasant one. We decided to continue and hope to reach Charaña by nightfall.

Leaving Corocoro was difficult, for we had a steep and rocky hill to climb before we could get out of the gully in which the town rests. After a few futile attempts, we made a long, fast approach at the incline and just managed to struggle the bikes over the top. Once up, there was not much to see. The low, barren, rolling hills soon flattened again into the desolate altiplano. There was no sign of a road — just a few llama tracks and footprints stamped in the dried ground.

Our compass was our guide. Far off to the west, we could see the snowcapped peak of Mount Illimani, which we used as our temporary destination. We began to worry, for we had a fuel capacity of about two hundred miles at sea level under normal driving conditions. Grinding through the altiplano at 14,000 feet, this distance was greatly reduced. We had no idea how far we would have to travel, for our wanderings were totally dependent upon the quality of the terrain. We picked our way through the streams and gullies.

Our greatest concern, however, was the expanses of loose sand that we came upon.

Tremendous flooding of the streams and rivers had deposited layers of sand across the land. Deposits were often up to a quarter-mile across, presenting many problems. Because of the depth of the sand, we had to push each bike across separately. While pushing, we would leave the engine running, engage the clutch, and spin the rear tire for traction. This was tiring; worse, it was a waste of fuel.

We saw no one, not even an Indian, for hours on end, and had little idea of where we were, but we could frequently see the snowcap of Mount Illimani. Occasionally, we could see the rest of the Western Cordillera standing solemn and cold, the majestic snowcapped peaks dominating the scene.

We came to a river — a deep one, much too deep to cross. Presented with the decision of which way to go, we chose to travel south and hope for a shallow place to cross.

Luck was with us in the form of an old suspension bridge with a roadway of dry, rotted beams. On our side of the bridge, scratched into the stone support, was the message, "Condemned, pedestrians stay off."

We had no choice but to cross. Cautiously, we selected the

better beams and threw the others aside. We ended up with a collection of beams that, arranged side by side, was slightly longer than the length of one of our motorcycles.

Slowly, moving each beam in turn from the rear to the front, we started to cross the bridge. Concerned that the combined weight of both bikes side by side across the span would jeopardize the structure, we moved one bike at a time in this manner.

As it was, three planks snapped beneath the weight of the rear tire of Dave's bike, but the frame caught on the remaining boards, and we eventually made it. It took several hours to complete the dual crossing, but time was of little concern. What was important was that the bridge signaled that we were back on the proper path. On neither end of the bridge was there any sign of a road, but we did pick up the familiar llama tracks.

A few miles from the bridge, we came to a small village populated by a few Indians who, as usual, spoke a language other than Spanish. The settlement consisted of just a few mud-and-rock dwellings and had the familiar odor of open sewage mixed with smells from the open kitchens. Where they got the wood to stoke their stoves was a mystery to us, and they had to carry water from a stream about five hundred yards away, but they seemed to be content.

As we pulled into the village, a scene unfolded similar to one from a Clint Eastwood movie. Fifteen men encircled us at a distance, while the women peeked through doorways of nearby huts. As we all stared at one another without uttering a word, Dave and I shared a very unsettled feeling.

Finally, we decided to attempt communication. Through the

use of improvised sign language, they pointed out the direction to Charaña. It did not look good. Again, we were left to make our own trail, continuing to head for the mountain in the distance.

A number of miles out of the small town, we came to an immense sandy area, about two miles across. We hesitated for we knew it would be a tremendous waste of gasoline. Nonetheless, we had no choice but to cross, and we spent several hours pushing both bikes across, one at time. The rigors of the physical exertion and the altitude were getting to us. It was a comforting feeling to reach the other side, climb onto the saddle, and once again head across the altiplano.

Late in the afternoon, we drove to the top of a hill to try to get our bearings. Thoroughly lost, we scanned the countryside. We saw what looked like a church, the cross barely showing over the next hill. Excited and confident that we had finally found civilization, we roared down the hill toward the church.

It appeared to be a town of about five hundred people, but a thorough search of all the huts convinced us that the town had been abandoned. There was no life evident anywhere. We walked out to the graveyard, and there learned the sad story of this forgotten town.

An epidemic apparently had struck the town, for skulls were piled around the church's altar and many skeletons lay in the corners of the graveyard. Some leaned against wooden crosses used as grave markers, as if a spouse or family member had wished to die next to a loved one already buried.

Darkness had fallen by the time we walked back to the town,

While lost in Bolivia, we came across a town that apparently had been wiped out by an epidemic. Skulls and skeletons lay everywhere throughout the cemetery.

and we decided to sleep in the abandoned schoolhouse. It got cold that night — very cold. The temperature and an eerie feeling resulted in a sleepless night. We pondered, shivering all the while, how the poor Indians could have adapted to life in the cold, wind-swept altiplano of Bolivia.

Morning came slowly, but we were up with the sun for fear of freezing to death in our bags. Our decision where to go was simple. To the left was east, the opposite direction of our destination. Ahead was a terrain that was impassable, and to the right was a deep gully. So we retreated. When it was possible once again to head west, we did.

Nervous about our fuel supply, we tried to conserve by coasting down hills. By midafternoon, we came upon a large river, well over two hundred feet across. We did not want to waste fuel driving along the river looking for a shallow spot, and from our vantage, the river did not seem to narrow in either direction. We tested the river's depth and found it to be about four feet deep. Even though the day was bright and sunny, it was cold in the high altitude, and we knew it would be tough to dry out our gear.

Replacing our riding boots with tennis shoes, we made several crossings of the river, transporting everything we did not want to get wet. We didn't want the bikes to get wet either, but we had no choice, so with a splash and a sputtering of the engines we attempted to drive as far into the river as we could (which wasn't very far). Most of the afternoon was spent pulling the bikes through the river (most of the way they were totally submerged) and then drying them out on the other side.

About four in the afternoon, I ran out of gas. A sense of total despair overcame us, but we did think that we were nearing our destination. We estimated that Dave had enough fuel for about five more miles in his tank. So he headed for the top of the highest accessible hill. Off in the distance, he spotted our destination town, coasted down the hill, and drove toward the town. His engine coughed and died of thirst about a mile from the town. Taking his spare fuel can from the luggage rack, he walked into Charaña.

Not much happens in Charaña. This small border town consists of a few hundred inhabitants and like so many other similar towns has no industry or visible means of support. A small retail trade services the natives who scratch a living from farming the high country. The town is desolate and the people destitute.

When Dave came walking into town with his empty gas can,

The customs station at Charaña.

he created quite a stir. Word spread like wildfire. People came running from shops and dwellings and assembled in a circle around him. They talked to one another, but no one would talk to him. He stood there silently staring at the populace for quite some time before a man in a uniform broke through the crowd and approached him. At first, Dave thought he was with the army, but as the man approached, his uniform become recognizable as that of the border police.

He addressed Dave in Spanish with a low growl in his voice.

"What is your name and what are you doing here?"

"My name is Dave Yaden. I am an American who has been traveling through Bolivia with a friend. We have been touring on motorcycles and we ran out of gas about five kilometers out in the altiplano."

The border guard looked skeptically at Dave and demanded that he produce his passport. Dave responded, "My passport is with my belongings which are still on the motorcycle out there," pointing in the direction from which he had arrived.

"A road has not existed in that direction for over ten years and the terrain is impassable. Now, where did you come from?" the guard demanded.

In front of the crowd, which was growing larger by the minute, Dave tried once again to explain his situation. He finished by asking, "What would I be doing walking around in this part of the world with nothing but a gas can if I weren't telling the truth?"

The guard pondered that statement for a moment and replied, "All right, I'll tell you what we are going to do. Juan here [he pointed to a teenager in the crowd] is going to take your gas can to the Panagra weather station and fill it with fuel from the generator tank. Then he is going to bring it back here. I'd have him accompany you back to where you say your friend is, but I am afraid some harm might come to him. So I'm going to let you go by yourself. If you do not return, then I'll assume someone else will have to deal with you. If you do return, then I want to see that passport."

Dave reassured the guard that he would return within the hour. With his filled gas can in hand, he started walking back to where his motorcycle was parked on the open altiplano. A number of small children began to run after him, but the guard put an authoritative stop to that when he yelled at the children to come back.

As he walked away, Dave glanced behind him and saw that

A Bolivian child tends the family herd. His sandals are made of tire treads and inner tubes.

the crowd was still standing there staring after him. That's natural, he thought to himself. A gringo walking into town out of nowhere is bound to intrigue the residents. Like so many others in so many similar towns throughout South America, the world these people knew ended just a few miles from their homes. If they had heard of the United States at all, they did not know where it was or anything about it.

As Dave walked, occasionally shifting the heavy gas can from one hand to the other, he reflected on some of the situations we had encountered that summed up this view of the world.

At one point, on the Central Highway between Cuzco and La Paz, we had come upon a brand new Ferguson farm tractor that was stuck in a pool of water just off the highway. It was angled into the pond with the dual front wheels apparently buried in the muck. The front half of the tractor, including about half of the engine, was under water. The first signs of rust were beginning to show through the paint. We talked to a farmer who later told us that the tractor was the gift of los Estados Unidos (the United States) and that no one knew how to drive it.

On another occasion, we purchased fruit from a vendor in a farmers' market. The fruit was handed to us in a paper bag printed with the words "Donated to the people of this country by the United States of America." The vendor did not know where the United States was, nor even much of a notion that it even existed. She did, however, appreciate the food donation. She was also a sharp vendor — she sold the bag to us for a nickel.

Dave put a gallon of fuel in his bike, then returned to get me. Putting the balance in my tank, we headed back to Charaña to face the border guard. About an hour had passed since Dave had left town with the fuel. As the late afternoon sun began to drop in the sky, the familiar chill settled into the air. From what Dave had told me, I suspected we were in for trouble trying to leave Bolivia and get into Chile.

We drove directly to the border guard station. Many of these remote border stations were open only certain hours of the day, and any traveler who arrived while they were closed had no choice but to wait until they reopened. The border guard was still there, although he had hung the "Closed" sign in the window.

"I didn't expect you to return," he said.

"First of all, I told you we would. Secondly, there is nowhere else to go," Dave responded.

"Let me see your passports," he demanded.

Dave and I handed him our passports and were surprised when he threw them into his top desk drawer and locked the desk. We protested.

"What are you doing? You can't confiscate those passports. You have no grounds."

"I have all the grounds I need. You two come riding out of the altiplano claiming you traveled from La Paz. That is impossible — there is no road. Now, I don't know what's going on here yet, but I'll bet that a search of those motorcycles will result in contraband, probably drugs. You just had some tough luck running out of gas and had to stop in here to refuel. What you did not count on was running into me. And you are going to pay for that mistake."

We had no choice. He had our passports, and as it was getting late, we decided to wait until the next day to clear up the whole matter. There was no hotel in town, but there were a couple of rooms behind the restaurant. Even though the room was dingy and cold, it felt good to eat a regular meal and to be inside. Once again, we spent a sleepless night and morning came slowly.

We were at the border station before the guard. In fact, he was a half-hour late arriving to open for the day. We assumed this was normal, for the only traffic he had was deliveries out of Tacna, Peru. No other roads into or out of Charaña led anywhere.

"We've been waiting for you. We're anxious to get moving. We'd like those passports, please," Dave said.

"I told you last night that I think something is funny here. I am convinced you gringos are smuggling something. So let's have a look through all of that gear," the guard responded.

He made us remove everything from the bikes. Suitcases were opened and inspected, all our clothing was searched, and the bikes themselves were scrutinized. He and his two compadres spent two hours tearing apart our stuff. Finally, nothing was left to search.

"I don't know how I managed to miss it. I know there is something here," he claimed.

"We told you yesterday that we are merely trying to get from one place to another and that there is no foul play involved. Now may we please have our passports so we can be on our way?"

We badgered him for another few minutes and he finally, reluctantly, handed us back our passports.

"Be on your way then," he said, "but your troubles are not over. This road leads to Tacna, Peru, and you do not have visas for Peru. You used them already and cannot re-enter once you are stamped out. I'll check you out of Bolivia, but you are going to have some fast talking to do once you get to the Peru-Chile border. They are going to want to know how you got into the country."

"Let us worry about that. Just give us the passports and we'll get going."

He handed us our passports and sneered at us as we drove under the control gate. Once out of sight from the border station, we pulled over to discuss our plight. He was right. The road led back into Peru, and if we followed it, we would be in that country illegally. We had the Western Cordillera of the Andes ahead of us, preventing us from blazing a trail.

Our campsite consisted of our small mountain tent protected by a motorcycle on either side.

There was one other option. A railroad track between Charaña and Arica, Chile, had been laid years ago to haul copper from the mines around Charaña. Those mines had been closed for years, and we assumed the tracks had also not been used since then.

We decided to give the tracks a try. Not only would it save us time, but we would be able to pass directly into Chile. We would have some explaining to do, but felt it would be easier than illegally re-entering Peru.

From the point at which we stopped, we could see the tracks across the plain. Reaching them was easy. Once on the tracks, however, the going got tough. The shoulders of the track bed had been neglected and portions had eroded to the point that we could not continue.

We decided to try riding between the tracks, but after just a mile knew that idea would not work. The track bed had settled, and the railroad ties were sticking up well above the gravel level. The one mile we had attempted had been brutal on the bikes. We decided to return and take our chances with the road.

The road was actually in pretty good shape. It wound around the mountains for mile after endless mile. And the view was magnificent. As the dirt road rounded the mountains with the inevitable switchbacks, panoramas were provided of the coastal flatlands and the Pacific Ocean. The starkness of the blue sky and the ocean contrasted with a brilliant white which signified that soon we would be traveling through the bare sands of the Atacama Desert.

Shortly after noon, we crested the Andes and started our descent to the coastal desert. By early afternoon, we had entered Peru, gaining an hour of time in doing so. Actually, although there were no indications, we thought we had entered Chile for a few miles. The borders of Bolivia, Chile, and Peru meet at one point, and because of our direction of travel, it seemed likely that we had touched the country of our destination.

Winding our way out of the mountains soon became a repeating choice of which road to take. The farther down the slope we traversed, the more roads there were to choose from. Signs were nonexistent. We would reach a fork in the road and have to decide which direction to follow.

Apparently, our decision-making was pretty good, for by late afternoon the road was starting to flatten out and the terrain was turning desert-like. We began to see a few vehicles on the road and sensed that the Peru-Chile border was nearby. We were beginning to feel pretty good about the whole situation.

Our euphoria was cut short. Dave and I were discussing how we were going to get across the border into Chile. We had a choice of approaching the border station and attempting to explain our situation, or of running the border at some point in the desert and then trying to explain how we arrived there to the Chilean authorities. Within a moment, the discussion became moot.

As we debated our options, a police Jeep with four officers rounded the bend. Their destination was not in question. The Jeep roared down the road, billowing dust and sand in its tracks, and came to a screeching stop, sliding sideways across the road just in front of us. All four officers bailed out of the Jeep, their rifles held at the ready. They immediately surrounded us, and the spokesman started his spiel.

"Step away from those motorcycles."

Dave and I put the kickstands down and dismounted.

"Stand over here," he bellowed, pointing his rifle to a spot closer to him and more distant from the bikes.

We obeyed.

"Let me see your papers, gringos."

We knew we were in trouble. We had not uttered a single word and yet he knew that we were Americans, or at least North Americans. It was obviously a setup. We deduced that the border guard in Charaña had shared with the Peruvian police his belief that we were not only illegally traveling in the country, but that we were probably smuggling drugs as well.

We retreated to the bikes to produce our passports. As we did so, the four policemen, in unison, aimed their rifles and tensed. We stopped in our tracks and turned to the spokesman.

Dave said, "I don't know what the problem is here, but we are harmless and prepared to cooperate with you fully. But please lower those rifles. You do not need to question us at gunpoint."

"Let me be the judge of that," the policeman responded. "Just produce those documents."

Dave and I went to the packets containing our official papers, with the rifles trained on us the whole time. My hands were shaking as I extracted the watertight packet from its compartment on the motorcycle.

Although we had lived peacefully among the South Americans for several months, we knew that they could be merciless to law-breakers, particularly foreigners. We were in Peru illegally, suspected of smuggling drugs. We had every reason to be concerned.

We handed our passports to the spokesman. He flipped rapidly through the pages and returned his gaze to us.

"I see where you entered Peru several months ago and then left the country as you entered into Bolivia. Although you are stamped out of Bolivia, you failed to have your passport stamped as you re-entered Peru. Let me see your visas."

We did not have visas, and he knew it. Dave responded, "It's a long story as to how we got here, and I'd like to tell it to you. But the fact is that we do not have visas to re-enter Peru. We have not passed a customs station since entering Peru and —"

The policeman cut off Dave in mid-sentence. "I don't want to hear this story out here in the middle of the road. We are going to lead the way into Tacna, and I want you to follow us. If you do not follow directly behind our vehicle, we'll shoot you. Plain and simple. Do you understand?"

Of course we understood. He had the guns and our passports. I got the impression that he was hoping we would try something stupid just so his men could use us as target practice.

"Yes," we responded, "but there is no need to treat us as common criminals."

"As far as I'm concerned, there is," he retorted.

The spokesman drove the Jeep, and he appeared to take delight in traveling as fast as he could down the dirt path, raising as large a cloud of dust in our faces as possible. At one point, we could not take the dust any more and began to drop back. He slammed on the brakes, sliding to a sideways stop as he had at our original encounter. We caught up with him, and he reminded us of his seriousness. Stay with him, or his men would fire. That was all he needed to say. We rode in his dust cloud for many miles before we reached pavement.

We followed the Jeep as the surroundings changed from rural to urban. As the driver wound his way through the streets of Tacna, his colleagues' rifles stayed trained on us the entire way. The Jeep slowed and turned into a compound protected by large stone pillars on either side of the driveway and a steel grate fence bounding the perimeter. A plaque on the stone entrance pillar read "Police Academy, Tacna, Peru" and below that another plaque stated, "National Police, Precinct XXIV."

The Jeep screeched to a halt, just in front of a main building in the compound, this time throwing off balance the two policemen in the back of the vehicle. One of them lurched forward, dropping his rifle as he grabbed for something to hold on to. The gun clattered to the ground behind the Jeep, and the driver jumped out of his seat and yelled some obscenity at the inept officer.

We pulled up alongside the Jeep, parked our motorcycles, and took off our jackets and gloves. The sun was setting, and it looked like a long night lay ahead.

The spectacle of the Jeep roaring into the compound with rifles trained on two trailing motorcyclists created quite a stir. A number of policemen (they may have been cadets) quickly surrounded us and were all talking at once, trying to find out what was going on.

The driver demanded that we follow him and instructed his three assistants to make sure we complied. We forged our way through the crowd that had gathered and made our way up the wooden steps of the compound's main building.

The two-story stone structure had wooden floors that creaked as we walked to the staircase. On the second floor at the end of the hall was a door with the nameplate "Lt. Gonzales." The driver ushered us into the office, leaving his assistants in the hall.

Inside the office, another policeman was sitting at the desk.

"My name is Lt. Gonzales," he said.

To the driver, he said, "Che, please see that these gentlemen take a seat there."

He pointed to two wooden chairs facing his desk. We sat, feeling a little more comfortable with the lieutenant's demeanor.

"I am led to believe that we have just captured a couple Americans trying to smuggle drugs out of Bolivia," said Lt. Gonzales. "It is not every day that a police lieutenant in lowly Tacna, running a training academy, discovers such a big catch. This may bring my name to prominence in Lima."

Upon hearing of his selfish interest in our case, our comfortable feelings quickly dissipated. Suddenly, the chairs felt very hard.

The lieutenant asked for our papers, and the driver handed them over. Lt. Gonzales performed the same ritual as Che had done back on the road, flipping quickly through the passports, and observing that they had not officially been stamped to re-enter Peru.

"Where is your visa?" he asked, looking directly at me.

In my broken Spanish, I answered, "You know by now that I do not have one. You also probably know the reason why I do not have one."

My impertinence apparently showed, for the lieutenant jumped to his feet and said loudly and indignantly, "I know that you are illegally in my country, and that there is probably some wrongdoing involved. This is an important case for me, and I am going to find out what that wrongdoing is. If it involves drugs, you will both be in a Peruvian jail for a long, long time."

We were beginning to get the picture. Our "capture" could make international news, and this lieutenant was intent upon capitalizing on the arrest. We were fearful that some obscure police cadet was at that moment planting a stash of cocaine on our motorcycles. If that were the case, then the lieutenant was quite right; they would railroad us into a cell for a long time.

He sat again as he continued, "Now, we have some very incriminating circumstances. You are in this country illegally with no papers. You entered from Bolivia. And how you got to Charaña is a mystery because the only road leading there comes out of Peru. You'd better level with me as to what is going on."

Dave spoke, "Look, Lieutenant. We are just a couple of guys traveling around South America on motorcycles. We needed to get from La Paz to Arica, or at least somewhere in Chile, and found that we had to re-enter Peru in order to do so. By the time we discovered the re-entry situation, it was too late to do anything about it."

"You can not get from La Paz to Charaña. There is no road. Now I want the whole story, and I want it straight," the lieutenant admonished.

Dave went into a long monologue, from the beginning. He explained to the lieutenant about planning the trip and the progress we had made up to La Paz. From that point forth, he went into more detail about the decision to make the drive to Charaña. He covered the daily details over the last several days and concluded with the Jeep intercepting us on the road. His last statements referred to our complete innocence.

The lieutenant listened intently, sitting through the nearly half-hour dissertation without moving, his elbows resting on the chair's armrests and his hands meeting in front of his body, corresponding fingertips touching one another.

"It's a good story, and plausible, I suppose," he stated. "However, I am not going to be satisfied until your belongings have been thoroughly searched. In the meantime, I consider you to be prisoners of the state, and you will be incarcerated until judged."

Dave and I were dumbfounded. Could this really be happening? And what were we going to do about it?

He instructed Che to deliver us to the impound cell. But before we exited the lieutenant's office, we made one last request.

"In our country, we get one phone call before incarceration," Dave said. "Are we afforded the same courtesy here?"

The lieutenant looked up from his desk and nodded to our escort. "Allow them one call, Che. And make sure it's a short one."

As Che led us down the hall to an office with a phone, Dave and I quickly consulted. "Who are we going to call?" Dave asked.

"I don't know," I responded. "I suppose our best bet is someone at the embassy in Lima. The only guy we know is Mitchelson and we didn't have much luck with him before, but we'll have to put our trust in him now. Calling anyone at home will do two things. First, it will scare the hell out of them. And secondly, it would take forever for them to get down here and get us out of this. These people do not know what bail is and we're going to be in here until someone with some influence gets us out."

It was well after quitting time at the embassy and we were concerned about reaching anyone at all. The switchboard put us through to the proper extension. Naturally, Mitchelson was not in his office; however, his secretary was. She was a beautiful women, in her early twenties, married to one of the attachés. We had joked with her on the several occasions that we were in the embassy waiting for our papers to arrive, and had developed a good relationship. Quickly we explained our situation and pleaded for her help. She replied that Mr. Mitchelson would not be in the next day, a Thursday, but that he would return on Friday. She would do everything possible to help us out.

Almost before I had the phone in the cradle, Che was ushering us out the office door. The fact that he could not understand my conversation with the embassy apparently agitated him. He pushed us on our shoulders as we started down the hall.

"Take it easy, Che. We are not going anywhere. You don't have to push," I stammered.

"Just get going. I don't have all night to wait on you two. I want to get home," he said.

Che led us out of the building, picking up his three friends as he reached the bottom of the steps. They still had their rifles at the ready. We headed toward the rear of the compound, which appeared to be about the size of a city block.

In the middle of a clearing, just short of a high concrete wall stretching across the back of the yard, was a single building with four doors. Each door had a small opening in the center about shoulder high to Dave and me. Four vertical steel bars were evenly spaced across the opening.

One of Che's assistants produced some keys, two of which opened the doors to the center cells. The doors swung open into the yard. Che gave a long sweeping motion with his arm, a mocking gesture for us to enter our new homes. He invited us into separate, adjacent cells.

The cell was dank, dark, and very cold. A light bulb dangling from the ceiling illuminated the interior — a single cot stretched against one wall and a broken toilet. Hunching on the dirt floor, I reflected on our plight and felt only desperation.

Now fully dark outside, I screwed the light a couple of times to turn it off. I stretched out on the cot and began to get nervous thinking about what might happen if Mitchelson did not respond to our plea. I also began to understand and believe some of the stories I had heard about the plight of convicted drug smugglers, particularly foreigners, rotting away in South American jails. But I also knew that, since we were innocent, we would eventually be released. I just hoped no one planted drugs on the motorcycles.

Realizing that I was not familiar with my surroundings, I turned the light back on. I attempted to talk to Dave, but the concrete walls separating the cells were too thick for conversation.

Some earlier inhabitants had apparently tried to dig their way out, for the dirt along the wall had many holes. I stuck my hand into one of the holes and realized the problem — under six inches of dirt there was a concrete floor. I once more turned the light out and lay down on the bed, my thoughts filled with apprehension about what might happen the next day. Somehow, I managed to fall asleep and did not awaken until well after daybreak.

The next day passed slowly. The only natural light in the room was what little sunlight could enter through the barred opening in the door. I had to leave the lightbulb on in order to see. It didn't make much difference, though. They gave us nothing to read and there was nothing in the small cell worth looking at.

Dave and I tried communicating, but the only method that worked was talking very loudly to one another through the door openings. No guard was assigned to keep an eye on us, but each time we started talking it attracted the attention of passing cadets, who would come over and stop our conversation.

Twenty-four hours had passed since our incarceration, and no one had spoken to us. Rations were brought twice a day, but the server uttered not a word.

On top of everything else, the cell was very dirty. It smelled awful because the toilet did not work, and bugs and rodents were everywhere. Rats, cockroaches, and a variety of spiders apparently called it home. We needed to get out in the worst way.

We pleaded with the servers to let us make one more phone call or to let us talk to someone in charge, but they remained tight-lipped.

Two days passed.

On the afternoon of the third day, we heard a commotion coming from the direction of the main building. I bolted to the opening in the door. To my amazement, I saw Mitchelson striding toward the cells with Che and an army of police cadets in his wake.

As he rapidly approached, we heard him command Che to have someone unlock the doors to our cells. Che turned and spoke to an assistant who broke into a run in our direction. The locks were released and the doors opened just as Mitchelson arrived.

I couldn't get out fast enough. Bursting into the sunlight I felt as if I'd been reborn. The feeling of not being enclosed and the emotionalism of the moment was overpowering. A brief moment passed with Dave and me standing side by side staring at Mitchelson, wondering what would come next.

His serious, angry expression was broken by the slightest up-turn at the corner of his mouth. He couldn't hold it any longer. Breaking into a wide grin, he exclaimed, "You guys look like hell!"

"We feel like hell. Can we get out of here?"

"Shortly. We have to have some papers signed. And there is the matter of officially re-entering you into this country."

As we walked back to the office, I asked, "Why did you come to our rescue so soon?"

"My secretary insisted on it. She's more than a secretary to me — she's become a friend. And her husband is a close associate of mine. Anyway, she implored me to get involved immediately. She said that whichever one of you called sounded desperate."

"But you were out of town when we called," Dave mentioned.

"I returned the following afternoon. Then it took me about twenty-four hours to contact the authorities here and find out what had happened. After they explained your plight, I was kind of curious myself to find out what happened. But I guess we'll deal with that in due time. Right now, it's important that we get you guys checked out of here."

We had walked up the steps of the central building and were headed toward the lieutenant's office. Before we entered, Mitchelson spoke.

"I want you two to let me do the talking. We have a delicate situation here. Gonzales thought he had a chance to be a national hero by capturing you two. I went way above his head for this release, and he is not at all pleased by the whole development."

Inside the office, Mitchelson said, "Lieutenant, I have here the necessary release papers from your governmental office in Lima. If you would be kind enough to sign them, as we discussed earlier, we can execute the visa matters and be on our way."

Gonzalez said, "Not so fast, Mr. Mitchelson. We suspected these gringos of smuggling and have not fully completed our search of their equipment."

Mitchelson replied, "You've had three days to conduct your search. A half-hour ago, you had the gas tanks removed and stuff lying all over the place. I saw it. At the time, no one said anything about contraband. Now let's get on with this. I don't want to call your superior in Lima, and you don't want me to either. Just sign the papers, stamp them properly, and we will get out of your way."

Lt. Gonzalez reluctantly signed and stamped the documents and had us escorted to the area where the bikes were impounded.

As we approached the fenced area holding the gear, our hearts sank. Our gear was scattered everywhere. Our suitcases had been removed, and all our belongings were scattered about the yard.

But worse, the motorcycles had been partially dismantled. The gas tanks, tires, seats, and other easily removed parts were lying around the frames. We were heartbroken. However, the damage wasn't so severe that we could not fix it. Mitchelson demanded tools from the police, and after several hours of reconstruction, we were ready to ride again.

While we were putting the bikes back together, we explained in great detail to Mitchelson the sequence of events leading to our problems with the police.

At one point, he commented, "You guys don't know how lucky you are. All they had to do was plant some cocaine in your equipment and there would have been nothing that I could have done to help you. Had I called them and told them I was coming that's probably exactly what they would have done. And I suspected that. So I brought one of the Peruvian nationals who work for us and had him stand guard over your equipment when we first got here. Gonzalez didn't like it, but we had written permission from Lima for the action. Short of that, I think you'd both be in jail for a very long time."

Dave said, "You know, when we were in Lima a few months

ago, we had some misunderstandings and left the embassy upset at one another. What made you decide to get down here and help us so fast?"

Mitchelson said, "I told you about my secretary. She's important and I listen to her. Also, it's my job. You're Americans and I am assigned here to, among other things, look after the best interests of our country and its constituents. But most importantly, we had a dispute regarding some mail you claimed was sent to our attention in your behalf."

Reaching into the inside of his suit jacket, Mitchelson extracted an envelope, still unopened. Handing it to me, he said, "We did have it. Apparently it was thrown onto a desk and slid off the back side, against the wall. A few days ago, we moved some furniture and found it sitting there propped up against the base of the wall. My apologies."

I responded, "No apologies necessary. You have more than made up for that insurance document being misplaced. You have no idea how grateful we are to you."

As Dave and I got our equipment back in order, Mitchelson said that he had to leave for the airport. We shook hands, and he got into the back seat of the car waiting for him. Dave and I hit our kickstarters and followed him out of the police compound.

Although it was late in the afternoon, we decided to head for the border. It was just a short drive, and after finding our way out of Tacna, we reconnected with the Pan-American Highway, which at this point was paved all the way to the border.

Our papers now in order, we crossed the border into Chile with little delay.

chapter fourteen
Chile

The Atacama Desert stretches through northern Chile for hundreds of miles. The desert is one of the world's driest regions, bounded on the west by mountains along the Pacific coast and on the east by the Andes. The elevation is high for a desert — above 2,000 feet — and consequently cool. But rain, and therefore vegetation, is nearly nonexistent. Arica sits at the northern end of this arid Chilean desert, just across the border from Peru.

After our experience in the Peruvian jail, we felt we owed ourselves a night of comfort, so we checked into one of the nicer hotels in Arica. A shower and a hot meal did feel good. But after our days in captivity, all we could think about was putting some distance between ourselves and the border.

Morning did not come too soon. We jumped on the bikes and barreled for our destination 1,500 miles to the south. Both the weather and the road were good. A clear blue sky contrasted with the barrenness of the desert, where not a stick of vegetation grew for mile after mile. I suppose to residents of the region the landscape might be monotonous, but to us the desert's starkness was beautiful.

We enjoyed our days in the desert. Each morning, we awoke to crisp air and a bright blue, cloudless sky that lasted throughout the day. The morning chill gave way to moderate afternoon temperatures that were very pleasant for our type of travel. We imagined that the few people who lived in this desert would consider anything less to be a disappointing day.

As a matter of fact, after several days in the desert, we were getting used to the climate and were beginning to think that way ourselves.

What kept amazing us was how stark the desert was. We could not see a tree or any living thing for mile upon mile. The white and tan desert sands had long ago hardened into permanent dunes. Not a breath of wind blew, and the sand on the flat valley floors between the huge dunes was packed so hard that it was as good a road as the road itself. In many places, all that distinguished the road from the rest of the terrain was a small border of sand that had been piled along the side of the swath created by a road grader's blade.

Many times we found the roadbed to be bumpy, like a washboard. In those instances, it was better to drive off the road and onto the desert floor itself. The tailings from the road grader guided us in the right direction.

The afternoon sun was not hot, but it shone so brilliantly that it was difficult to distinguish where the side of the road turned into the desert. Normally, bumping over the tailings would signal

The Atacama Desert in northern Chile is one of the driest spots in the world. Stretching for hundreds of miles, it is very desolate.

that we had crossed from road to desert. But occasionally the tailings were missing, having been flattened for some reason. Perhaps the road grader had missed a spot or another vehicle (of which we saw very few) had experienced the same problem, and we crossed over to the desert surface in its tire tracks. At any rate, if we were not constantly looking for the tailings, we might suddenly find ourselves off course and have to search for the road.

Long stretches separated the desert towns, so we had to be cautious about having enough gas to get from one fueling stop to another. As had been the case along most of the trip, there were no service stations. Houses were the fueling stations, and they had no distinguishing markings. They were located approximately every fifty to one hundred miles along the road, and we just had to ask where they were. Fuel was pumped from a fifty-five-gallon barrel into a two- or three-gallon container and then poured into our gas tanks. Obviously, some of this gas had been in the barrels for a long time. We were always cautious to put a cloth screen over the opening to our fuel tanks to catch the sediment and larger impurities that were inevitably present.

In the evenings, we would merely drive off the roadbed a few hundred yards and plant the tent in the openness of the desert.

Night after night passed with a stillness and quietness that was almost disturbing. It was so quiet that even my own breathing became annoying.

We had beans for dinner one night, and I developed a mild case of gastric distress. Well into our night's sleep, I very audibly blew some wind, startling Dave so badly that he jumped up, nearly flying out of his sleeping bag. The tent was small, just big enough for the two of us to squeeze into. As he bolted upright, he caught the top of the tent with his head and pulled the supporting stakes out of the ground. No harm was done, but we did have to reset the tent.

Day after day passed. What had once been interesting terrain was becoming monotonous. We encountered few people and even fewer vehicles. We often saw mirages. Usually, these took the appearance of a body of water shimmering in the distance, beckoning us to travel just one more mile to embrace its liquid coolness.

Once we saw what appeared to be a dark spot on the desert well ahead of us. This "mirage" did not disappear but continued to materialize. As we approached it, we began to recognize it as a truck in the roadway.

It turned out to be a dump truck which had, for some unknown reason, ended up on its side in the middle of the road. The road was straight and smooth, as it had been for the last several hundred miles, and we had to assume that the driver swerved the truck violently and it overturned.

As we drove up to the vehicle, the seriousness of this accident took us by surprise. Three men lay squashed underneath the truck. One was crushed by the dual rear wheels, and two were lying under the rim of the dump truck's bed. Apparently, they had been riding in the bed of the truck, and when it overturned they were catapulted against the side of the truck bed. As it rolled onto its side, they were crushed by the rim. How the one man ended up beneath the wheels was a mystery.

These three were obviously dead. We decided to look for the driver. The driver's door was pinned beneath the overturned truck, and we had to climb on top of the cab in order to open the passenger door. Glancing down into the cab, we could see two people. The driver was on the bottom, pressed against the inside of the door by the passenger resting on top of him. The passenger was breathing but unresponsive, so he was either in shock or unconscious. We could not yet determine the condition of the driver, although he was not moving.

I decided to climb into the cab to see if we could extricate the two. I had to be careful where to step in order not to slip onto the passenger. I stepped in, resting my left foot against the side of the driver's seat, followed by my right foot against the side of the steering column.

First, I checked to see if the driver was alive. Feeling for his pulse in his neck and his wrist indicated that he was not. However, he may have been in deep shock. Because of our awkward positions, I did not want to jump to a hasty conclusion.

The next task was to try to remove the passenger. I hadn't had much first aid training, but I did know that we had to be extremely careful. Checking him over led me to the conclusion that he was okay except for one problem. I could not see a portable radio in the cab, but apparently there was one, for its antenna was impaled through the middle of the passenger's right thigh. The broken end was serrated, and I saw no way to pull it out. Our problem was how to get this guy out of the cab without further harm.

Dave and I worked for an hour. No one came by. As slowly and as carefully as possible, we lifted the passenger up through the door. Getting him down to ground level was just as difficult as getting him out of the cab. All the while, we had to be careful of the antenna sticking through his leg.

After extricating the passenger, we were able to examine the driver more closely. There was no doubt — he was dead. Now our full attention was directed to do what we could to ensure the passenger's survival.

We had a small first aid kit with us and attempted to make the man comfortable and to stop the bleeding. What we needed was some help. We were discussing the possibility of one of us driving to the next town for a doctor when we heard a motor off in the distance.

It seemed to take forever for the sound to get close enough for us to see the vehicle, but finally a bus came into sight, rumbling down the sandy roadway loudly popping and banging,

Accidents were common, but this one in the Chilean desert was particularly gruesome.

expressing its lack of a muffler. Its brakes were also obviously in need of work, for it screeched to a halt just in front of the wreck. Normally, these buses were packed with people, many of them standing in the aisles and occasionally sitting on top of the bus where the luggage was held. But this bus was only half full. Even so, Dave and I wondered where these people were coming from and going to out in the middle of this desolate desert.

The passengers immediately scurried off the bus to get a closer look. In other circumstances, it would have been humorous — twenty people pushing and shoving each other to get out the door as if the rear of the bus were on fire. But they all disembarked, circling the wreck, talking rapidly, and pointing at the men thrown under the truck. After they had satisfied their curiosity, they formed a circle around our patient, whom Dave and I now had resting on the ground on our sleeping bags, which we had doubled up for his comfort.

The driver approached us. "What a terrible accident. What happened?"

Dave responded with a brief recap of our appearance on the scene one hour earlier and our efforts to aid the victims. He ended his short account by saying, "This man is the only one still alive, although he remains unconscious. We need to get him to a hospital. Is there one anywhere nearby?"

The driver told us, "There is a doctor who runs a clinic at Iquique. That is our next major destination. If we can get him onto the back seat of the bus, then I can have him there within an hour."

Dave said, "Okay, we'll help you get him onto the bus, but if you see anyone else on the road, please ask them to have the police come as soon as possible. We'll stay here at the accident site until further help arrives."

Six of us lifted the injured man and cautiously moved him to the long seat at the back of the bus. It was a little tricky maneuvering him with the antenna sticking through his leg, but we managed to get him situated for the ride ahead.

This episode took about half an hour, but the driver got his passengers reloaded (with a few of them to watch over the victim) and headed for Iquique. Although we knew the bus made a lot of noise, it still startled us when the driver hit the starter. The engine cranked over three or four times and came to life suddenly with a tremendous bang. It sounded like a cannon had gone off. Naturally, Dave and I were standing right behind the bus. Not only did our hearts jump when it fired, but it belched a cloud of thick black smoke all over us. We later wondered what had possessed us to stand behind that bus.

The bus rumbled off to the south, and we could hear it well after it disappeared from sight. We waited. Help was slow in coming. Now, without our patient to occupy our thoughts, we began to feel remorseful. We sat and looked at the crushed bodies under the truck and began to talk about how precious life is. Our philosophical discussion took our minds off the disaster and helped to make the time pass more quickly.

Two hours went by before a police convoy of three Jeeps and an ambulance arrived at the scene. By that time, darkness was beginning to settle. The captain of the entourage questioned us about our knowledge of the incident. After half an hour, as they were still retrieving bodies from the wreck, Dave and I followed the direction of the bus, south toward Iquique.

The accident stuck in our minds for a long time and had a sobering effect on our driving for the next several days. We did not discuss the episode much, and several weeks passed before we mentioned it to a third party.

Time has a way, however, of changing one's perspective. Several months later, we were describing the accident scene to a friend. Dave surprised me by his humorous anecdote of the survivor's leg injury. He was telling, in great detail, of our arrival on the scene and our search for survivors. He said, "I cautiously, but quickly, climbed up the side of the overturned truck and peered into the cab. Keith was right behind me. I said, 'Oh my God,' and Keith asked what was wrong. I turned to him and stated, 'It's the worst case of an-aerial disease I've ever seen.' "

We drove south through the desert for several days. The scenery was monotonous, but the ride was not. Well, in a way it was. The road, hard-packed and ridged like a washboard, stretched out forever through the sand. The uneven surface of the road sent the bikes skittering. At times, we felt more comfortable riding across the open desert than the road itself. But we never tired of the ride. We knew that every mile of this adventure would be remembered as a once-in-a-lifetime experience, and we savored every minute.

We enjoyed nearly two weeks in the desert. The dilapidated amalgamation of metal, wood, and stucco that made up the few towns along the Pan-American Highway enthralled us. We spent much time in them, talking to the inhabitants about their lives.

What we saw was pretty bleak. These towns had no industry, functioning merely as service centers for the few buses and trucks passing through. Very few people worked, yet these towns had grown to, in some cases, several thousand people.

It was depressing, yet the people seemed content. Somehow, they managed to eke out their meager existences in these massive slums which lacked public water or sewage systems, spending generation after generation in complete obscurity and continuing squalor.

We took many side trips. The desert is rich in deposits of sodium nitrate and copper, and we visited several of the mines. Occasionally, we would bump into an American working in the area as a consultant. We looked forward to these encounters as they always provided stimulating conversations and usually free meals.

The free meals were needed. We were running short on money and long on time. By our original schedule, we should have arrived in Pucón, our ultimate destination, about three weeks earlier, and we were still several weeks away. In letters home, we had told of our tardiness, hoping the information would be passed on to the Pucón city officials.

We were not, however, concerned about our delays. This was a once-in-a-lifetime trip, and we wanted to make the most of it. Any guilt over our delayed arrival in Pucón was always pushed to the back of our minds.

The bikes had been running well. We stopped every couple of thousand miles to change the oil, adjust the valves, clean the carburetors, and so forth. Occasionally, we dealt with more serious problems, such as a broken clutch cable, a plugged carburetor jet, or dirty fuel with no reserve fuel filter. This time, it was a flat tire that we could not seem to fix.

Fortunately, we were in the town of Chañaral when the flat first occurred. I patched the tube three times before buying a new one. The new one went flat as well. We figured there must be something wrong with the tire, but repeated inspections showed no problem. We messed around with that tire most of the day before we finally found a two-inch nail embedded sideways through the tire tread. It was not visible when the tire was loose, but when the tire was remounted and the tube inflated, the internal air pressure would cause the tube to press on the tip of the nail, popping the tube.

We traveled south for a couple of days, usually pitching the tent and cooking over an open fire. Sometimes, we would stop in town for a meal but were constantly concerned about our finances, so we ate sparingly. Besides, the restaurant food did not always agree with us.

We arrived in the small town of Copiapó early one evening and decided to find a decent meal. We entered a typical small restaurant with a whitewashed stucco exterior with "Paco's Restaurant" hand-painted in blue letters over the arched door. We made the mistake of ordering the house special. Paco brought us a smelly concoction that looked like some sort of seaworm with a special seaweed sauce. Since we ordered it, we had to pay. Not wanting to pay for two wasted meals, we tried to eat it. That was a mistake; the stuff was awful. Getting past the smell of a forkful was tough enough, and swallowing was even tougher.

All the while, a piano player and a drummer were attempting to entertain the diners, which consisted of Dave and me. So this was Latin music! Neither musician knew, or apparently cared for that matter, what the other was doing. The drummer beat out his rhythms as the piano player played at a different tempo. We couldn't determine which was worse, the meal or the music.

Time took care of the decision. We left the music behind, but the meal traveled with us for several days. Dysentery returned for a fourth episode and made motorcycling miserable.

We felt lousy, but the terrain and the highway improved. Leaving the desert behind, the countryside began to turn green — not like a jungle, but more Mediterranean or dry summer subtropical.

The road was mostly hard-packed dirt with sections of well-used pavement which almost made the dirt portions more desirable. Through some sections near Antofagasta, a new highway was being built paralleling the old. Most of it was paved, so naturally Dave and I drove on it where possible. The crews put rocks and piles of dirt across the new highway at quarter-mile intervals to discourage travel on these "not-yet-open" sections, but that didn't stop us. We drove over the dirt or around the rocks and continued on. It certainly worked to discourage four-wheelers, though.

The closer we got to Santiago, the more the terrain changed and the road conditions as well. The road began to climb once again into the mountains. As soon as we left the flat valley floors, the roads deteriorated. It was as if the government worked only on those portions of the road that were flat and straight. The surface became very rough with rocks showing through the hard-packed dirt surface.

Weather conditions began to match those of the road. A heavy mist settled against the mountainside, not quite a drizzle but heavy enough to saturate the dust that we raised. We were particularly uncomfortable when it clung to our eyeglasses. Above 5,000 feet, we would break out of the fog into bright sunlight, only to dive back into the mist.

Finally, fifty miles from Santiago, the road turned to smooth pavement and remained so all the way into the city.

Forty miles from Santiago, we saw a group of thirty motorcyclists approaching us. As we neared, they spread across both lanes of traffic, forcing us to stop on the road's shoulder. They also stopped, and a spokesman stepped forward.

They were members of a Santiago motorcycle club who had been expecting our arrival for two months. They had been alerted to our journey by some people from Pucón, our destination to the

south. We enjoyed an escort into Santiago, surrounded by motorcyclists riding all kinds of machines.

We had finally made it — Santiago, our last major city, the
place so far off that never seemed to get any closer.

We found the city to be beautiful and impressive with its many
tall buildings and wide, clean boulevards. We also found it to be
quite formal, seldom seeing anyone dressed in anything other than
a suit and tie or nice dress. Even the street people looked out of
place without a jacket.

And so Dave and I became the subject of gawkers, with our
well-worn jeans, leather jackets, and motorcycle boots. We certainly felt out of place, but did not have much else to wear.

The Chileans were especially intrigued by my beard, bright
red and several inches long. Verbal comments were restrained,
but I certainly received some interesting glances from passersby.

We had several days worth of errands to catch up on in Santiago
before heading south, so we took a fairly decent room in the downtown São Paulo Hotel.

The ensuing days consisted of matters primarily related to our
return trip. We had anticipated shipping the bikes back to the United
States from Santiago. Having purchased our return passage, we
needed to make arrangements for the motorcycles.

We found a shipping company that was willing to take a de-
posit on the bikes and to crate and store them for us. The idea
was that upon returning to the states, we would send money to
have them shipped back. It was a risky business. We felt the chances
of never seeing the bikes again were moderately high, but we had

no choice. We were rapidly running out of money and had a long journey ahead of us yet. We would be in Chile for a few more weeks. Fortunately, we were holding passenger ship tickets from Santiago to Panama and airline tickets from Panama to Miami.

The five days we spent in Santiago were exasperating. We had to deal with embassies, shipping companies, airline carriers, the Chilean government, newspapers and radio stations that wanted interviews, U.S. citizens wanting to talk to us, the Peace Corps, etc. We were not used to all the attention and busy schedules. Whenever possible, we would jump on the bikes and escape to the mountains for a few hours of sightseeing. But even that pleasure was cut short when we had to deliver the bikes to the shipping company for crating and storage.

While in the hotel in Santiago, we decided that since we would be walking and taking other forms of transportation from this point forth, we should perhaps reduce our luggage to one suitcase apiece. The embassy was willing to hold our sleeping bags and excess baggage until our return from Pucón.

In our sixth-floor hotel room, we took everything out of the suitcases and rearranged things in some order of priority. The weather would be turning cold and wet as we traveled south, so all the hot-weather clothing was packed in the suitcases for storage.

Having removed everything from the bags, I noticed that a lot of dust and dirt had built up in their hinges and recesses. Dust flew from the side pockets when I snapped the elastic. I determined that the best thing to do would be to shake the suitcase upside down out of the window. This would jar loose the dust and it would blow away in the breeze.

Well, it was a good plan and worked accordingly, except that I failed to notice that my spare pair of glasses was still tucked into the pocket in the lid of the suitcase. As I shook the suitcase out the window, the glasses plummeted six floors onto the sidewalk below. From my vantage point, I could see that there was no sense in going to retrieve them. Upon impact, they shattered into what appeared to be several pieces. I hadn't needed them on the whole trip and therefore believed that I would be okay without the spare pair. I hoped that would be the case, for I am extremely near-sighted and nearly blind without them.

Our financial woes were beginning to cause grave concern. We had just purchased round-trip train tickets from Santiago to Pucón, leaving us with fifty dollars in cash between us. Our fares back to Miami were already paid, but we still had a month of traveling ahead. We also had to get from Miami to Portland. We could not work to earn money because our visas prohibited it, we didn't know anyone here from whom to borrow, and we were too proud to write home for a loan. So we decided to tough it out. We had a few utensils, clothing, and equipment we could sell but decided to wait until our return to Santiago to worry about that.

We purchased tickets on the Rápido leaving for Valdivia. As luck would have it, we were late arriving for the train and had to take the slower, older one. It rattled and banged its way down the tracks for fifteen hours. We finally arrived in Pucón late the next afternoon where we were greeted at the train by the local dignitaries.

The mayor of Pucón, along with his city council and half a

dozen other people, were standing on the platform as we stepped off the train. Although it was a Saturday, they were dressed in their Sunday best, and we felt very out of place. We had decided to wear some slacks and sportshirts that we had been hauling all down the continent, but it did little to make us appear more presentable. The clothes had been stuffed in suitcases for months and were permanently creased in the wrong places. On top of that, we had been wearing them for twenty-four hours, most of that time riding on the train.

Worst of all, we had both lost more than forty pounds, and the clothes hung on us like extra-large on a skeleton. Furthermore, we had long since discarded our nice shoes since we did not want to carry the weight. So we wore our motorcycle boots and tried to improve our appearance by pulling the pants legs over the boot tops. We were a sight to behold.

Rain was falling, and the wooden platform was slippery as we stepped off the train. Our greeting party was standing close to the two steps leading down from the door of the train, and we nearly slipped into a handshake with first the mayor and then the other dignitaries. Two of those greeting us spoke English, but with translations of the pleasantries it took several minutes to get through the introductions. They had umbrellas and raincoats, but Dave and I stood in the rain trying to act excited about our new acquaintances. They soon, however, realized our wet discomfort, apologized profusely for having kept us standing in the rain, and quickly paraded us to the small train station at the end of the platform.

Once inside, we were more affable and able to carry on a conversation. They had everything planned. Raul Gonzales (one of those who spoke English) was to be our host, and we would stay in an upstairs bedroom that his children had vacated when they got married and moved out of the house.

An itinerary covering four days was planned, and it sounded like we were going to have little free time. Although we were looking forward to a little rest, we understood. We were the only visitors other than exchange students to make the journey, and the first to travel there by land. The small town had been looking forward to our arrival and wanted to make our stay fulfilling and memorable.

We left the tiny train station and piled into the back seat of Raul's Jeep. The other passenger was Jerry Smithson, a Peace Corps volunteer headquartered in Pucón but who was spending most of his time in the mountains helping to educate rural Chileans.

A short ride from the station took us to town, which we passed through on the way to Raul's house. But it was long enough to get a feeling for the countryside. Everything was green. Grassland spread over rolling hills that extended in ever-increasing size to the east. Many pine trees spotted the hillsides in clumps that gathered into forests on the more distant slopes. It reminded us a lot of Oregon. It was similar in climate, except that the seasons were reversed. Pucón was leaving the winter doldrums and entering a rainy spring.

Unlike the countryside, the town was not at all like its sister city in Oregon. Much smaller than Lake Oswego, Pucón consisted of a downtown section of just a few square blocks. The road from the train station to town, and throughout the downtown section, was paved. Other than that, the roads were dirt and we could see the muddy tracks left by vehicles in the side roads scattered throughout the area.

We had looked forward to getting here for months, but now that we had arrived we felt melancholy. This was the turning point of an adventure that we were not ready to end. Furthermore, we did not feel entirely comfortable with our new responsibilities. We had been motorcycle bums for six months, and all of a sudden we tried to become diplomats, carrying forth the greetings and official representations from the government of Pucón's sister city. We felt and looked out of place. Our baggy slacks, motorcycle boots, and leather jackets were in stark contrast with the wool sweaters, wing tip shoes, and raincoats that our hosts sported.

The first order of business was to stop at Raul's home and take our bags inside. Jerry seemed to know his way around, for he grabbed our suitcases and darted through the rain from the car to the front door, tripping the door latch with his right index finger while pushing it open with his knee. By the time we entered the house, he was descending the stairs empty-handed.

The house was comfortable, a small two-story home consisting of three upstairs bedrooms and a common bath. The downstairs was one large room, partitioned into a family room and a kitchen. The family room was homey with dark wood paneling on the walls and hand-hewn beams across the ceiling. A large stone fireplace in one corner of the room provided heat for the entire house. Throw rugs were scattered across the wooden floor, upon which an overstuffed couch and several chairs were situated.

The kitchen, which opened onto the family room, was large

enough to place a small dining table at one end. Cooking was done on a large cast-iron wood-burning stove that dominated one wall. The other wall of the kitchen was taken up by a long counter, interrupted in the middle by a sink.

Raul was obviously well-to-do by Chilean standards, and we later learned that his hardware business was one of the town's focal points.

Except for the stone fireplace, the entire house was made of wood. We discovered that virtually everything in southern Chile was constructed primarily of wood; there was an abundance of it. Paint, however, was not plentiful. Everything was natural wood with no preservatives or coloring. This lack of surface protection was taking a toll; many of the buildings had been constructed years before, and the wet weather was slowly destroying them.

No one was at Raul's home, and we wondered where his family was. Raul seemed to be in a hurry, suggesting we rush upstairs, freshen up after our long train ride, and return downstairs. In an effort to find out what was happening, we called Jerry upstairs and asked him what was going on.

"Jerry, what's the problem? What's the rush?" I asked.

"These people have been expecting you guys for months," Jerry said. "This is a big deal to them. They've planned a banquet today in your honor down at their equivalent of the grange hall. Being Saturday, everybody in town is going to be down there."

"What are we expected to do?" Dave queried.

"Well, nothing really. It's just an opportunity for the towns-people to throw a massive party. They want you to feel comfortable in your short stay here and thought this would be a good introduction to the community. You know, the local politicians will say a few words, and then everyone will end up eating and drinking all afternoon. Incidentally, I should warn you. They love to drink wine here, and they have a local variety that they will amply ply you with. Be cautious. It tastes harmless enough but packs one hell of a wallop. And these people are hard to say no to."

Since we were already wearing the best we had, we washed our hands, splashed some water on our faces and headed back downstairs. Jerry and Raul were standing by the door.

"Ready to go?" Raul asked.

"Yep."

"I guess Jerry told you that we have a welcoming ceremony planned. I didn't want to tell you about it before because we wanted to surprise you. There will be a lot of people there, and I hope that you don't feel uncomfortable with this."

Raul spoke in Spanish, although his English was pretty good. "Not a problem," Dave responded. "Actually, a good meal and some company sounds great. I've been talking to myself and to Keith here so much over the months that some other conversation sounds like a good idea."

I could relate to Dave's statement. We had spent a lot of time together in hotel rooms and particularly in the tent. At times, we had run out of things to say to each other. But beyond that was the solitude. Riding a motorcycle leaves you with only yourself to talk to. That can be both good and bad. We both had had enough of each other and ourselves and welcomed outside conversation.

The Jeep plowed through the muddy streets as we made our way to the community hall. The rain continued to pelt the vehicle with such force that the canvas top could not resist it. Water forced its way through the fittings and seals, creating little cascades of drips. We had to rearrange our positions within the Jeep to avoid getting soaked. But it was a short drive and the discomfort of the ride soon ended.

The hall was tucked against a knoll so stuffed with pine trees that they intertwined. Some of the trees at the base of the knoll could not gain a full footing and as a result grew diagonally, some so acutely that they hung precipitously over the hall's roof.

The hall itself was a large barn-like building and, like every other structure in town, made entirely of unpainted wood. Broad-leafed meadow grass surrounded three sides of the hall, giving way to the pine trees at the rear of the building.

Except for the muddy road leading to the entrance, the entire picture was green and gray. The heavy overcast sky deluged the countryside with gray sheets of rain, bleaching out the old unpro-tected boards while at the same time feeding the forests and meadows, turning them an even deeper green.

The Jeep slid to a stop as close to the grange hall's entrance as possible. Jerry, Dave, and I got out, while Raul parked the car. We waded through about twenty feet of sloppy mud to the small concrete slab in front of the door. A line of cars extended down the far side of the roadway. Judging from the number of footprints in the mud, a large crowd was gathered inside. As we stood on the concrete pad, protected from the rain by a small canopy, we could hear a constant roar inside, like a hundred people all talking at the same time.

"Sounds like some of the locals are already pretty well warmed up for this occasion," Jerry said.

"When did this thing get under way?" I asked.

"Well, it wasn't supposed to start until about half an hour ago, but by the looks of it, some of the townspeople got here a little early to get a head start on the wine jug."

"Is that going to be a problem?" I asked.

"No," Jerry replied. "Some of these people are notorious for getting a little carried away. They do it all the time, so they should be able to handle it."

"Well, I hope they don't expect it of us. We don't drink very much and having lost so much weight, we're vulnerable," I said.

"I think that's going to depend upon your constitution," Jerry replied. "These people will be expecting you to imbibe, because they think it is socially proper to do so. The problem is, it sounds like some of them have a head start. They enjoy a good time, and it may involve them thinking you are having a good time, too. Translated, that means they'll try to get you drunk. Good luck."

Our conversation ended as Raul splashed through the mud in huge steps, apparently thinking that the fewer steps he took, the less mess it would make. But each time his foot landed, mud splattered all over his pants legs. He had had to park the car quite some distance away. By the time he reached us, he was dripping wet and spattered with mud. It didn't seem to bother him though. He was eager to get inside and drink wine with his friends. Besides, he was used to the rain and mud — it was a part of life.

We entered the hall, Raul first, followed by Jerry and then Dave and myself. The thunderous conversation took just a few moments to die down, followed by an eruption of echoing applause. We were confused, but Jerry leaned over and shouted in my ear, "They're glad to finally see you here. Let the party begin."

The building appeared much larger inside than it had appeared from the outside. Maybe it was because of all the people crammed into it. Picnic-style tables were lined from one end of the hall to the other on a wooden floor, with very narrow aisles separating the rows. There must have been five hundred people in the building.

At the end of the structure were several kegs, some containing beer but most holding wine. Apparently, each section of the tables had an appointed "runner" who kept the jugs filled, for there seemed to be some organization to what looked like mass pandemonium. It smelled good standing inside the building. Next to the kegs were several tables laid out with different kinds of salads and meats. Most of the food had been prepared hot and was by now cold, but it still smelled good.

No one, however, was eating anything. All attention was focused on the liquor.

The applause died off, and the roar of conversation once again dominated the building. Two of the city council members who had greeted us at the train station approached and shook our hands again. One of them took Dave, and the other myself, and spirited us off in different directions.

I was taken about midway down one of the center aisles. I lost track of Dave.

The council member pushed aside a couple of citizens, and he and I climbed onto the bench that was attached to the table. He attempted to make some introductions of those immediately surrounding us, but there was too much noise for any of us to hear one another.

We shook hands and bobbed our heads at one another. Before I was fully seated, someone handed me a glass and filled it to the brim with white wine. It was a large glass.

I do not remember eating dinner, but everyone said I did. In fact, I don't remember anything after the second glass of wine. The first order of business was a toast by the person to my immediate right. That was followed by a toast from the person to my left, and then the person sitting across the table, and so on. These were rapid-fire toasts, none of which I could understand, or hear for that matter. What was I supposed to do? These were toasts in my honor, so I was sociable and drank to the toasts.

I was awakened the next morning not by the smell of the bacon and eggs being prepared for breakfast (that made me feel nauseated) but by the clatter accompanying the breakfast preparation. I felt awful.

My head was pounding to the rhythm of a cerebral jackhammer, and my mouth felt like it had been stuffed full of cotton soaked with castor oil. I rolled over to reach for my glasses on the nightstand, and my nose scraped on something hard on the pillow. I'm so nearsighted I have to be right on top of something to see it. And I was right on top of this — dried blood.

I started feeling around on my body and soon found the source. My beard was caked with blood and large sections were missing. My stomach sank to my toes, and I desperately grabbed for my glasses so I could inspect the damage in the mirror. But my hand came up empty. I felt all over the nightstand to no avail. I sat on the edge of the bed and felt around on the floor. No glasses.

Dave's bed was about fifteen feet across the room. I could make out a blurry lump under the covers. I shook the lump, and Dave emerged from under a pile of blankets.

"Geez, Dave, I feel awful. And I can't find my glasses. Help me look for them, will you?" I said.

"They're not in the room, Keith. You lost them last night. With the condition you were in, I know you won't remember, but you had quite an experience last night. Matter of fact, I wasn't far behind you in the wine-drinking contest, but I am happy to announce that you beat me hands down. I don't feel too good myself, but you must feel like hell. And incidentally, you look as bad as you must feel."

I sat on the edge of his bed and tried to focus on him, but he was still blurry. "So what happened? Why can't I find my glasses, and why is my face so bloody?"

"Well, I didn't see all the action myself. Remember, we were sitting in different parts of the hall. But Jerry and Raul filled me in on the details as we rode home in the car. That was supposed to be a nice party yesterday, but I guess some of the locals showed up a little early and got too big a head start on the wine. By the time we got there, the festivities were well under way."

"Yes, I remember that. And I remember having a couple of quick glasses of wine during the toasts," I said.

"That was the beginning of the end for you. I was watching your table from my place across the room. You didn't have any women sitting around you, and those guys fueling you weren't holding back a thing. Fortunately, the ladies sitting at my table brought some restraint to the guys.

"Anyway, apparently the town's barber was sitting across the table and down a few seats from you. Raul said the barber kept talking about that long, bright red beard of yours and how he would like to have a souvenir of it. The night continued, he kept drinking, and he kept talking louder and louder about your beard.

"Sometime after dinner," Dave continued, "he recruited a few of his friends — those guys across the table from you who kept your wine glass full — and they led you to a small office at the back of the hall. Three of them held you in a chair, while the barber came after you with his steak knife to extract his souvenir of your beard.

"They were all drunk, and I guess it took a while to get what he wanted. All the while, you were squirming and doing your best to resist in your drunken stupor. As a result, he stabbed you in the face several times as he was whacking at your beard. I have to say that if his purpose was to make you look horrible, he certainly succeeded."

Sitting on the edge of the bed, my mind was reeling. I was trying to remember some of the episode, without success. All I knew was how lousy I felt. My head was pounding, my stomach was turning somersaults, I couldn't see, and my beard was butchered. All I could think of was the saying I had heard somewhere, "It always feels so much better the day after the day after." That's what I wanted, to turn the clock ahead so I could feel better, see again, and have my beard grow back.

"What about my glasses? Where are they?"

"I don't know," Dave answered. "Jerry noticed last night when you stumbled into the house that you didn't have them on. We think you had them when you got into the Jeep, but we're not sure. We looked around the Jeep last night but thought we'd continue the search this morning. You know, it's possible you lost your glasses when you tossed your cookies last night. We couldn't get you into the back seat so you sat in the passenger seat. And it's a good thing. About halfway home last night, you started to get sick and asked Raul to pull over. He hadn't even stopped when you opened the door and barfed all over the road. They could be lying out there somewhere."

"Terrific," I said. "I'm a couple of months and tens of thousands of miles from home, I can't see a hand in front of my face, I don't have my glasses, and my spare pair fell out of a sixth-story window onto a sidewalk. If we can't find those glasses today, we're going to have a delay we can ill afford."

"I know," Dave said. "But let's not get too concerned until we resolve the missing glasses issue. We may get lucky."

I didn't even try to make myself presentable for the breakfast table. I felt like hell and no amount of grooming would help. I pulled up a chair and sat with Raul and his family, along with Dave. They proclaimed how sorry they (and the entire town for that matter) were for the actions of the barber and his three cohorts. Some foreign visitors finally come to Pucón and one of them gets attacked with a steak knife. Raul carried on and on about the townspeople's disappointment over the incident.

I kept telling him that it was okay and to not be too harsh on my attacker. After all, it was the emotion of the event. But my reasoning did not appease Raul. I suppose my appearance didn't help. I was sitting at his breakfast table unable to see, with blood-shot eyes, dishevelled hair, and a ragged beard caked with dried blood.

After breakfast, the first order of business was to try to find my glasses. I didn't go because I was of no use; I didn't feel like it anyway. All I wanted to do was to lie down.

Raul and Dave decided to walk back along the road the Jeep had traversed on the return trip from the hall the night before. It was still raining and the road was muddy, Dave later related. But it was a worthwhile trip. They returned with my glasses.

They retraced the path to where Raul thought he had pulled over for me the night before. About twenty feet away, Dave noticed the two earpieces of the spectacles poking up about two inches out of the mud. They had fallen off my face, lenses first into the soggy roadway. A tire track running right between the two earpieces was barely visible, they both confirmed.

The townspeople had planned several activities for us over the next two days. Now that I had recovered my glasses, I had no reasonable excuse for not attending. The first thing I did was look in the mirror at the damage the mad barber had wrought. It was a mistake. My face looked bad enough, but the weight loss and 25,000 miles of dusty roads embedded in my skin added to an already ugly scene. I was a mess, with only one option – shave.

I borrowed a razor from Raul and, after washing the blood off, shaved the remnants of my beard. It was a sad day – not that I had a prize crop, but I had grown attached to the beard. I felt angry that I had to shave it for any reason other than my own choice.

Shaving was tough. Raul's razor had been used well beyond its reasonable life and, with the coarseness of my beard and the beads of blood I couldn't wash off, it was a painful procedure.

The beard finally removed, I did my best to make myself presentable. With my hair combed and smelly stuff all over me, I descended the stairs. Raul, Jerry, and Dave were standing in the kitchen drinking coffee. The moment I walked in, they all began to chuckle. Actually, Dave broke into a horse laugh. I thought at first it was because of my hungover appearance.

Dave said, "Thye, you look like walking hell. Maybe you should have left that beard on."

I tried to think of a snappy retort, relating back to Dave's version of a beard. But I passed on the opportunity, thinking that his comments to me were well-deserved.

Raul said, "We have many things to do over the next two days. Everybody in town wants a little bit of your time, so I have arranged a schedule that we should make every effort to keep. This morning, we meet with the mayor and the city council, and at lunch they have some presentations for you. In the afternoon, it's the city water plant, a tour out to the lake including the scenic route on the way back in.

"Then there is a dinner party at the house of Arturo Rodriguez tonight. Tomorrow we'll see the parochial school, the post office, watch part of a soccer game, and meet several people at Carlos' Cafe."

Dave and I glanced at one another, knowing that inwardly we were both feeling the same way. We were used to solitude and the excitement of the open road. Now that we had reached our destination we felt trapped, compelled to do what was necessary to make everyone else happy. But we also knew that it would be a short-lived commitment and we owed it to the people of Pucón. After all, we were the ones who had made such a big deal about this trip in the beginning, when we kept emphasizing the fact that our destination was Pucón, Chile. So for a few short days, we would play the part of the celebrity and be gracious guests.

In later moments alone, Dave and I were most grateful for the hospitality that was shown to us. What we really liked was the food. We probably ate more in our three days in Pucón than we had in the previous two weeks on the road. We also enjoyed not having to spend any money. For a day or two at least, our concern about how we would get home on fifty dollars was forgotten.

Lunch with the mayor and his council members was entertaining. Everyone did their best to speak English, but most were far from fluent and the discussion kept slipping back into Spanish. The mayor was a large, boisterous man with a trove of jokes that he kept spitting out rapid-fire. His jokes were even more hilarious because of the dual languages. He would try to tell them in English, stumbling along up to the punch line. Not sure of a joke's effectiveness in English, he would jump back to Spanish for certain words of which he was unsure. It did make a very entertaining dissertation.

At the end of the luncheon, the mayor presented Dave and me with identical hand-carved wooden plaques. They were about the size of large dinner plates and intricately worked. Around the edge, in two semicircles were the words "Lake Oswego, Oregon; Pucón, Chile; Sister Cities." A ring inside of this circle was carved with "Dave Yaden; Keith Thye." And on the inside of the ring was the date of our expected arrival: July 6, 1963. Above the date were the words "Moto Raid." Our motorcycle ride (Moto Raid) was carved in wood for posterity. The minute it was handed to me, I knew the plate would remain one of my prized possessions.

We carried out our appointed duties over the next couple of days with enthusiasm. As my hangover dissipated, I began to truly enjoy myself. The people of Pucón were terrific, and we found that they liked to laugh with us at life's experiences.

After viewing their water treatment plant, we drove up to the lake where the water originated. An old four-foot-diameter wooden pipe carried the water from the lake to the treatment plant. Many of the steel bands encircling the pipe had rusted and broken off, leaving weak spots in the pipe. Leaks had sprouted in many of these weak areas, and sections of the pipe looked like someone had used it as target practice with a shotgun. Water spurted all over the place. Rather than being embarrassed about their water supply, our hosts laughed heartily with us at the sight of this mile-long pipe wasting more water than it was delivering.

Our visit to Pucón came to a close. We had enjoyed ourselves and were sorry to leave. The townspeople had gone out of their way to accommodate us and show us a good time, and they had succeeded in both. We left Pucón with our wooden plaques, a Chilean flag, and an armful of native trinkets. More importantly, we left with a treasury of good memories.

The water supply for Pucón, Chile.

We caught the train back to Santiago and hoped to get some rest on it, for we had only one day before we were to catch the ship at Valparaíso. Naturally, the train was crowded and slow, and sleeping on the wooden seats was difficult. A train derailment in Lonoche held us up for two hours, making the trip a very uncomfortable twenty-hour ride back to Santiago.

Our last day on the continent of South America was a busy one. The first order of business was to go to the warehouse where the bikes were stored to check on their safety. From there, we went to the embassy to check on our mail and then to the consulate to see if we could borrow some money. No deal.

We went to the airline agency to check on our flight from Panama to Miami, and then to Gondrand Brothers, the agency holding the tickets for our voyage to Panama. Between taxis, buses, hotel rooms, and miscellaneous taxes and up-charges on tickets, we found ourselves in a desperate situation for cash. Our fifty dollars had dwindled to five, and we still had to get from Santiago to Portland, Oregon.

The docks at Valparaíso were a forty-five-minute bus ride from Santiago. Naturally, we were running late. At the bus station, we discovered we had missed our bus to Valparaíso, and the next one would not get us there in time to board the ship. We needed to come up with an alternate plan, and fast. We managed to locate three other people also going to Valparaíso and a cab driver who would take us there for fifteen dollars. So we all piled in. Once we got started, though, the cabby was such a terrible driver that we were not sure we would survive to see Valparaíso.

But he got us there. We arrived an hour before boarding time. We were now flat broke, without a penny to our names. We wouldn't need money on the ship, but realizing that we would need some once we arrived in Panama, we decided to visit a dockside pawnshop. We sold Dave's Canon camera, for which he originally had paid one hundred dollars two years earlier, receiving thirty-five dollars in exchange. We both carried cameras (one for slides and one for prints) but thought we could get more money for his.

chapter fifteen

The Reina

"The *Reina* is a large passenger liner which primarily cruises the western coast of South America, taking affluent travelers to various ports between Chile and Panama," the tourist brochure read.

What the pamphlet did not tell us was that these "affluent travelers" were but one of three classes of passenger on board the ship. Those well-to-do tourists were on the top decks, enjoying their shrimp cocktails and martinis. The swimming pools, shuffleboards, and activities were terrific, we were told.

Two middle decks were occupied by persons somewhat less prosperous, those who aspired to a wealthier lifestyle but could not quite afford it. They enjoyed most of the same privileges as the upper-deck passengers, but had a separate dining room and, understandably, a menu less epicurean than that above.

Dave and I knew this voyage would be difficult. After spending seven months on a motorcycle, neither of us looked forward to ten days of sedentariness on a ship. But we had made the decision in Panama to book passage on the *Reina* because it was the least costly means of getting back to Panama from Chile. Naturally, we opted for the "economy" package, which was substantially cheaper than the middle-class passage on the decks above us.

Economy class on the *Reina* meant just that — no frills. We walked up the gangplank to board the ship and, upon showing the crew member our boarding ticket, were abruptly escorted back down. He took us to a much shorter ramp toward the rear of the ship.

This time, we did not have to climb to get on board. The gangplank extended straight from the dock to the entryway into the ship. There was a long line ahead of us and much confusion among the crew trying to board all the passengers.

Dave and I had felt out of place in many circumstances on this trip. Often disheveled and covered with dust, we had tried not to be embarrassed when around more well-groomed people.

This company we were among now, however, made us feel right at home. We were with the working class and the farmers in whose company we had spent much of this trip. The situation at dockside was just as confused as if they were in their town square at home.

Everybody was talking at the same time, shouting and waving tickets in the air. We couldn't understand what was going on, other than mass confusion, and felt the best thing to do was just to hold our place in line. We had tickets and knew that eventually we would be shown to our cabin.

Actually "cabin" was a misnomer. We gradually inched forward in the line to be greeted by a crew member who would show us to our room. We never did find out what nationality he was, but he did his best to communicate to us in Spanish the accommodations of economy class. We knew we were in trouble when he pointed out the dining room. It was on the deck where we entered the ship, just barely above the water line. This meant that the sleeping areas were probably on an even lower deck, below the water line.

Sure enough. He led us down two flights of stairs and showed us to our cabin. It was more like a sleeping berth in an old Pullman railroad car. Two bunks were hinged to the wall, one above the other, to allow space to move around. Opposite the bunks were two narrow doors. They had to be narrow in order to open into the room without hitting the pulled-down cots. One door housed an adequate closet and the other a bath compartment.

It was tight. You could sit on the toilet, wash your hands in the sink, and stick your feet in the shower all at the same time. But at least it was ours and we did not have to share it with any other passengers.

Our berth was toward the inside of the ship, and therefore had no portholes. It did not make any difference anyway as we were below the water line.

Looking around the economy-class decks, we concluded that this section must originally have been designed for the crew. No self-respecting ship designer would intentionally lay out a passenger section like this.

Our only question was where the crew stayed. We later learned that they were crammed into two decks below us, into areas not originally intended for sleeping.

The stairways leading to the upper decks were locked. The powers-that-be at the cruise line did not want us to mingle with the upper-class guests. We all had one chance, however, to see how the other half lived. There was a required safety drill where we had to grab our life preservers and assemble at preassigned lifeboats. Since the lifeboats were on the upper decks, the crew had to unlock the stairways. One quick glance at how the upper-deck passengers were treated led Dave and me simultaneously to the same conclusion: we had to find a way to get up there.

It didn't take long. We knew that the ship had accessways that the crew used to move between decks, and we only needed to use these passages when they were unoccupied. We knew our usual attire would make us stand out on the upper decks, so we always walked around in swim trunks. Even this was conspicuous at times, though, because the weather turned nasty for four days. Some of the passengers must have thought we were crazy to want to go swimming in those conditions.

The ten days of inactivity on the ship were tough enough for us to endure, but would have been unbearable without the access to the upper decks. The activity rooms, the swimming pools, and particularly the library were popular with us. We even found a few books in English.

We also became big fans of the upper-deck buffets. The food in the economy section may have been fine for a South American farmer (and we had lived on that food for months on the road), but we got spoiled quickly when we saw the afternoon and midnight buffets that were offered upstairs. Chicken, fish, roast beef, pasta, salad — we soon found ourselves living on the top three decks and venturing below to our berth only to sleep.

But even with the finer aspects of cruise ship life, we grew bored. There was only so much swimming, reading, dominoes, and table tennis that we could handle. We were traveling, but it wasn't our preferred style.

About every other day, the ship would pull into a port to let off passengers and board new ones. The first was Antofagasta, Chile, where we had an opportunity to go ashore and explore the town. We walked from one end to the other, taking a few pictures and examining the ruins of an old iron smelter. We learned on this first port of call that it was going to be difficult to get to Panama without spending any money. We couldn't even afford a beer at a sidewalk cafe.

The next port of call was Arica, Chile, and the ship was loaded and unloaded by launch. It was interesting to watch the confusion among the crew as they attempted to load and unload luggage one piece at a time.

A thought suddenly struck me, and I wondered why it had not occurred to me before. South Americans normally try to accomplish tasks in the midst of confusion. I finally determined that it stemmed from a lack of leadership. Even when there was a leader, he usually did not know what to do either. Consequently, everyone involved in a task wanted it done his way, and sometimes it seemed to take forever to finish a job that could have been performed more quickly and efficiently.

Not going ashore in Arica did not break our hearts. We reflected back on Che and our jail time in Tacna, Peru. His presence just across the border made us fearful of running into him again. If he were to catch up with us, he would surely concoct some excuse to incarcerate us, and this time the embassy's representatives might not be successful in their efforts to extricate us.

It didn't take long for a few of the crew members to figure out our scam. We were sure it would be just a matter of time before we were discovered in the crew's stairway.

But in fact, we never were discovered there. They caught us lounging around the upper decks of the ship and recognized us as third-class passengers. Those crew members assigned to a specific group of guests attended to those passengers for the whole cruise. Those that performed functions such as bartending, however, might end up at any bar on the whole ship.

It was one of these guys who recognized us. We were sprawled on a couple of lounge chairs on the sun deck when he came by. In broken Spanish that was hard to understand, he asked, "Aren't you two guys staying down in the economy-class section? I could have sworn I have seen you down there."

My immediate reaction was to act dumb and deny the whole thing, but a quick mental review told me that a lie would only get us in trouble.

"Yeah, as a matter of fact we are," I answered. "But we've been going crazy down in that dungeon." (I elected not to tell him that we had been frequenting the upper decks already for the past three days). "We discovered one of your crew passages to the upper-class sections and decided to see how the other half lives."

"You know, that's a good idea," he responded. "I don't know why a lot of the other passengers don't try to do the same thing.

Well, maybe I do. I have been on this ship for two years and have found that most of the passengers, at least in the economy section, are very aware of a class distinction and will honor that position in life. Congratulations, and more power to you. Is there anything that I may get for you?"

Dave and I glanced quickly at one another, knowing what the other was thinking. We were mentally wiping the nervous sweat from our brows and beginning to realize that we had a friend who was willing to let us get away — even help us — with our charade.

"A Coke would really be great right now, but we can't pay for it," Dave said.

"In this section, soft drinks are free, but you have to pay for liquor. Down in the economy class, you have to pay for everything, other than scheduled meals. But I guess you already know that," he said.

"We know about economy class, of course," Dave said. "But we didn't realize the situation up here. If you would be so kind, we would appreciate a couple of Cokes."

"You've got it," he said.

Upon his return, we introduced ourselves. He did likewise and we learned that he liked to be called Alex in English. He was a Brazilian, and Portuguese was his native tongue, hence our trouble in understanding his Spanish. But that was fair; he seemed to have more trouble with our Spanish than we were having with his.

Although the crew was under strict orders not to fraternize with the passengers, we came to know Alex well. He was a young man of twenty-three years who came from a small town just outside of the new capital of Brasília. His family was a large one (nine brothers and sisters), and he considered himself the sibling patriarch of the family, not only because he was the oldest but because he had an excellent job which afforded him sizable respect.

Alex was a nice guy, and soon he had pulled three other of his colleagues into our friendship. The others were deckhands who also had access to the entire ship.

Dave and I later understood that we had become sort of folk heroes among the lowly crew members. It was not due so much to our invasion of the upper decks as it was to our willingness to get to know them. Dave and I had picked out a couple of lounge chairs on the sun deck that we considered "our spot." Each day, a number of crew members would stop by to say hello. They managed to keep our secret among themselves.

We stopped at the port of Callao, Peru, to exchange passengers. The stench that filled the air quickly brought back memories of many of the port cities we had passed through that had the same awful smell.

After a short walk through town, we decided to head to our lounge chairs on the sun deck to capture some sun without the ocean breeze. The weather was perfect — eighty degrees and calm — but the smell from town seemed to cover us like a hard rain.

I was in the lounge chair reading when I glanced up and saw a seagull flying low over the bow of the ship. Something must have been wrong with him for he ran head-on into a cable from the bow of the ship strung taut to a mast holding some electronic equipment about thirty feet behind the bow. The seagull careened, in a flurry of slapping wings, into the water between the ship and the dock. I could not see over the side of the ship from the sun deck, so I passed it off as a nearsighted seagull trying to execute a tight righthand turn and failing.

I went back to reading. About two minutes later, some shadows crossing the page I was trying to read made me look up. I saw a flock of seagulls, which must have numbered in the hundreds, and which was growing larger with each passing moment. There were so many birds that they were blocking out the sun.

Dave and I became concerned. Something was going on. We grabbed our towels and books and were just rising out of the lounge chairs when the birds let loose. I barely had time to wonder what had hit me in the hair before a gob of dribbly white stuff began trickling down the right lens of my glasses.

Those birds had declared war on us. By the time we were able to stand up, we had been barraged by the first wave of angry aviators. It was as if these birds had blamed the crash of their fellow seagull into the ship's wire on Dave and me. We dashed for the stairs leading to the next deck down, where we could get under cover. The birds continued to pummel us the entire way. In our wake was a trail of bird droppings no more than five feet wide. Those guys had good aim!

Once on the lower decks, the other passengers stared at us as we made our way through the sparse crowd. We had been alone on the sun deck, as most of the passengers were preparing for lunch. Some of the women pointed and gasped. We couldn't blame them; we must have looked pretty repulsive. Goo was dripping from every inch of our bodies and all we could think of was diving into the ocean.

We made our way to the gangplank, descended it (with people more than willing to step aside for us), ran down the dock to the stern of the ship, and flew off the dock into the salt water. Even the water smelled, but we didn't mind. It was the most refreshing plunge in the ocean we had ever had.

The cruise continued without any further major incident. We spent the days on the upper decks, returning below only for occasional meals and to sleep. We were worried that one of the ship's crew might kick us below, but we began to realize that we were now a fixture on this particular cruise, and the crew seemed to feel we were right where we belonged.

We crossed the equator, and the weather changed dramatically. It had been warm and sunny — very pleasant with a slight ocean breeze blowing across the decks. The morning after crossing the equator we awoke to heavy humidity which by noon had escalated to a stifling heat with so much moisture in the air we could almost wring it out like a wet rag.

At midmorning and late afternoon, almost like clockwork, clouds suddenly formed overhead and let loose a torrential downpour of rain. It would last only for fifteen or twenty minutes, and the heat would barely ease through the entire spell. We looked forward to these episodes as our daily showers and enjoyed lying on our respective lounge chairs through the spell. On a couple of occasions, the rain fell so hard that we had to take cover, as the drops stung when they hit our skin. It was as if they had been shot from a gun.

The closer we got to Panama, the more we began to wonder how we would reach Portland, Oregon, without some help. We thought we could probably spend a few days with Joe and Connie Young in Panama before we caught our flight to Miami, but then what would we do? We kept reassuring each other that things would work out somehow, before quickly changing the subject.

chapter sixteen

Panama

Ten days after boarding the ship, we cruised under the Thatcher Ferry Bridge and pulled into port in Colón. Clearing customs was much easier on the ship than it had been on the road, and a short time later we were walking down the road to Joe and Connie Young's house. About a half a block from the house, we saw a great big guy riding a motorcycle toward us. Joe arrived at his driveway about the same time we did.

I think we caught him by surprise. We had previously sent him the date of our arrival, and obviously he had forgotten it. But no matter, he said. He had offered us his home on our return trip and was glad to have us.

It felt good to be back in Panama. We had spent enough time here on the way down that we were familiar with the city and felt comfortable in it.

Our stay with them was during the middle of the week. Joe took his car to work, offering us the use of his motorcycle. The three days were busy ones. We spent some time at the embassy picking up and sending our mail, including twenty-five rolls of film, and reacquainting ourselves with the staff there. They did not recognize us because we had lost so much weight. Also, Dave had since shaved his unique beard, which on our earlier visit had been a topic of conversation.

Although we had paid for a flight from Panama to Miami, we needed to reserve seats on a specific flight. The balance of the time was spent roaming around town looking up friends we had met on the way down.

chapter seventeen
U.S.A.

Joe and Connie drove us to the airport and wished us well amid a last-minute session of hugging and handshaking. At the last call for the flight, Dave and I exited through the gate and walked across the tarmac to the plane. Ascending the portable stairway to the plane, I looked back one last time to wave to the friend who had helped us so much in Panama.

A weird, empty feeling developed in the pit of my stomach, and it remained with me as I settled into my seat on the plane. I wondered what was wrong but then realized that it was a melancholy feeling of loss. Dave and I had planned this trip for a year and had been on the road for more than eight months, and this was the last chapter. We still had some traveling to do, but the excitement of Central and South America was now behind us.

Our recent experiences would now transform into lifelong memories that would fade as the years rolled by. I was sorry to see the adventure come to an end, and this feeling in my gut was a manifestation of that.

The propellers sprang to life and roared mightily as the plane accelerated down the runway. The plane lifted into the air, and my feeling of sadness lifted with it.

We were traveling light. Each of us was carrying a mid-sized satchel with a few changes of clothes and some sundry and toilet items, as well as our sleeping bags. The rest of our stuff had been left with the bikes for shipment back to the United States, had been boxed and mailed from Santiago, or had been sold.

How far can two guys get with $6.10 between them? That was the question we contemplated on the plane. Our plan was to begin hitchhiking and go as far as we could. When our money ran out, we would have to wash dishes or mow lawns or something in order to raise a few more dollars for the next leg.

Our other problem was time. It was mid September, and we wanted to be home in time for fall semester, which started at the end of the month.

Standing in line to get through customs and immigration allowed us time to reflect on some of the remote customs stations we had encountered. We had to appreciate the civility and efficiency of the U.S. agents.

Stepping out of the airport into the humid Miami heat actually brought a feeling of relief. We were back on our home turf. Although we still had a journey ahead of us, we were comfortable in the sense that we were no longer in a foreign country.

We did not have any particular route that we intended to take. All we wanted to do was head in a general northerly direction.

As we walked down the sidewalk, away from the airport, we

noticed a food service truck backing up to a loading door. Imprinted on the driver's door was the emblem of the city of Fort Lauderdale. Approaching the driver, we explained our situation to him, and he agreed to take us to Fort Lauderdale with him when he finished unloading. After a short wait, we were headed north.

We asked for him to drop us off just as he exited the freeway so we could catch another ride, and he was happy to oblige. But we soon learned that rides on the freeway were few and far between. Eventually, a college kid picked us up and took us to Boca Raton. Since he dropped us off on Highway 2, the coastal highway, we decided to try our luck there. We soon discovered this was the way to go. With all the college kids traveling up and down the coast with their surfboards and snorkeling gear, hitching rides was not a problem.

It took the rest of that day and the next two days to reach Jacksonville. Once there, we lucked out. We had been standing alongside Interstate 10 for several hours when a construction worker picked us up. He was just beginning a week's vacation and was going to Baton Rouge, Louisiana, to meet his girlfriend. He had just gotten off work and was tired, but he was in a hurry. If we would help with the driving, he would take us the distance.

The 700-mile lift helped. Once in Baton Rouge, we thought we would head for Houston. We had a high school friend who was now attending college there and felt if we got that far, perhaps he would put us up for a few days while we earned some money to continue hitchhiking home.

But first we had to get to Houston from Baton Rouge. Our ride dropped us off as we exited the freeway just as darkness was setting in. Rain clouds had been gathering for the past hour, and a gusher appeared imminent. Under the circumstances, we decided to look for shelter. We crossed the freeway to a truck stop. Just as we reached it, the clouds opened up.

Sitting over a cup of coffee, we took stock of our situation. We now had two dollars left between us and a long way yet to go. We were very hungry, for we had mostly been eating oranges from roadside orchards and buying an occasional candy bar to tide us over. But what we needed most was a ride to Houston.

We waited for the rain to stop before venturing back outside. Even though it was dark, the air was still warm. We stood on the highway with our thumbs out for several hours to no avail. Nothing was going to happen tonight, so we went back to the truck stop and spread our sleeping bags on the asphalt under a semitrailer. The grass around the parking lot was wet, and we were concerned about more rain during the night.

We were abruptly awakened in the morning by the roar of the semi's engine. It startled us so much that we jumped up and hit our heads on the underside of the trailer. We scrambled out from beneath the trailer with our belongings just as the driver was dismounting from his cab.

We stared at each other for a moment, and he asked us what we were doing. We explained our situation and why we had slept under the protection of his trailer. He apologized for startling us.

Waking from a night in his sleeper compartment, he wanted to get an early start and had started the engine to warm it up. He was making a safety check before he started to roll. As luck would have it, he was headed for Houston and offered us a ride.

The driver was planning to stop in Beaumont, Texas, for a late breakfast. Because we would soon be in Houston and we were very hungry, we decided to spend our last two dollars. We did make certain, however, that we saved one dime for a phone call when we got to Houston.

We arrived in Houston about noon, and the driver was kind enough to drop us off downtown, since he had to go right through there anyway. Our first and only order of business was finding a pay phone. Because we knew that our friend lived close to the Rice University campus, finding his phone number was not a problem.

We did end up with one problem, though. I did not have a piece of paper to write on and relied on my memory for the phone number the operator had recited to me. I kept repeating the number over and over in my mind as I motioned for Dave to hand me our last dime. He did so, and I dialed.

"Hello."

"Hello. My name is Keith Thye. Is this the residence of Lovett Smith?"

"Who?"

"Lovett Smith. Look, is this 236-7491?"

"Sorry, you misdialed."

So now what do we do? We were flat broke and needed the help of a friend. But we had to reach him first.

Dave suggested that we each go in different directions and check the coin return box of every pay phone we saw. If one of us were to find a dime, he should make the call, and we would meet back at our starting point in one hour.

I found a dime in about the fifteenth phone I checked. I made the call — correctly this time — and reached Lovett. He said he would leave immediately to pick us up.

I returned to meet Dave, and within the hour we were gorging ourselves from Lovett's refrigerator. The afternoon was filled with telling stories from our journey.

Also that afternoon, we called home to let our folks know we were okay and that we would be home within two weeks. We needed to earn some money before progressing.

They said, "No way." They had been looking forward to our return and felt that we had done enough. They arranged to have tickets waiting for us at the Houston airport the next morning.

We did not protest.

We arrived home to a waiting crowd of friends at the Portland airport on a mild afternoon day in late September.